# THE DEAD DON'T ANSWER

Goldsmith crossed the carpet in two paces and rapped at the inner door. Again there was no answer, but the door was ajar.

He pushed it open. A faint, acrid smell tickled his nose and he sneezed.

This room was luxurious compared with the other. It contained a desk, a swivel chair, an armchair, two filing cabinets, curtains at the window and an Indian rug on the floor.

It also contained a body, face down on the floor beside the desk. Round about his right foot were the remnants of a smashed coffee cup and saucer. It looked as if he had forgotten they were on the floor by his chair, had risen, trodden on them and pitched headlong forward. His right hand, stretched out as though to break his fall, was convulsively clenched round the double element of an unprotected electric fire. That was where the smell was coming from. It was clear that the unfortunate man was dead. . . .

"Hill is rapidly taking over as the most civilized, clever and enjoyable crime writer we have."
—*The [London] Sunday Telegraph*

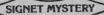
SIGNET MYSTERY

# REGINALD HILL

# A VERY GOOD HATER

A SIGNET BOOK

**NEW AMERICAN LIBRARY**

NAL BOOKS ARE AVAILABLE AT QUANTITY DISCOUNTS WHEN USED TO PROMOTE PRODUCTS OR SERVICES. FOR INFOR-MATION PLEASE WRITE TO PREMIUM MARKETING DIVISION, NEW AMERICAN LIBRARY, 1633 BROADWAY, NEW YORK, NEW YORK 10019.

SIGNET TRADEMARK REG. U.S. PAT. OFF. AND FOREIGN COUNTRIES
REGISTERED TRADEMARK—MARCA REGISTRADA
HECHO EN CHICAGO, U.S.A.

SIGNET, SIGNET CLASSIC, MENTOR, ONYX, PLUME, MERIDIAN and NAL BOOKS are published by NAL PENGUIN INC., 1633 Broadway, New York, New York 10019

First Signet Printing, February, 1988

1  2  3  4  5  6  7  8  9

PRINTED IN THE UNITED STATES OF AMERICA

Hatred alone is immortal ... We revenge injuries; we repay benefits with ingratitude ... We hate old friends; we hate old books; we hate old opinions; and at last we come to hate ourselves.

WILLIAM HAZLITT


Dear Bathurst was a man to my very heart's content: he hated a fool, and he hated a rogue, and he hated a whig: he was a very good hater.

SAMUEL JOHNSON

# PART ONE
## 1963

# CHAPTER I

"THERE HE IS!"

"Where?"

"Coming out of the lift."

Goldsmith looked with growing disbelief at the four passengers stepping smartly from the lift as though afraid the doors were going to close and crush them.

Unless there had been surgery involving age, or height, or sex, Templewood must mean the man in the light grey suit. He was nearly six feet tall, and had a rather longer than military moustache, greying hair to match his clothing and the air of confidence possessed only by the monied or the criminal classes. He looked about fifty and had kept himself in trim or knew a good corsetière.

"*Him?*"

"Yes."

Goldsmith relaxed for the first time in twenty-four hours.

"You're joking!" he said.

"No."

"Then you've bloody well flipped. *Him?* Just look at him! A man can't change that much."

Templewood was unperturbed.

"Twenty years does a lot. Here. Remember this?"

He produced from his wallet a dog-eared photograph. Five soldiers grinned broadly at the camera. Goldsmith looked from the young man at the left of the group to Templewood, who parodied the snapshot grin.

"I can tell it's you," he protested.

"That's because you know it's me and because I don't mind you knowing. You see me once a year at the reunion and I bet each year you think *Christ! he's changed*. I'll tell you something, Billy boy. I couldn't tell this was you if I didn't know."

His forefinger flicked the boy in the middle of the group.

"I was only eighteen. Unformed. He was a grown man."

"Listen, Billy, I haven't brought you here because I'm certain. I've brought you to help check out a suspicion, that's all. When I'm certain, I'll know what to do."

He glanced sharply at Goldsmith from under the luxuriantly bushy brows which he used to claim were partly responsible for his success with women. *They all want to have their tit-ends brushed with these*, he used to boast in the barrack-room darkness. Goldsmith, only a year younger by age but ten by experience, had listened to the stories with excited envy. What saved Templewood from being just another sexual braggart was an element of self-deprecation in his make-up; he salted his triumphs with tales of failure and fiasco which at the same time confirmed his unthinking assurance in his own virility.

"Is that what's bothering you, Billy? What to do if it is him?"

Goldsmith shook his head.

"I just can't see a single point of resemblance, that's all."

"Good. I hope you're right, I really do. Because it bothers me, Billy. I'm too old to want to start killing people."

They sat in silence now for a few minutes. They were in the entrance lounge of the Kirriemuir, one of the old hotels in the vicinity of Russell Square. The man in the grey suit had paused at the reception desk to pick up an evening paper, then made his way into the cocktail bar. Through the glass door they could see him perched on a stool reading his paper and taking occasional sips from a sherry glass.

"All right, Tempy," said Goldsmith. "I've seen him. And I'm bloody glad I was coming down for the re-union at the weekend anyway! What made you ring?"

The phone call had come the previous evening. He had not recognized Templewood's voice at first and the man had been so excited that he hadn't paused to give his name.

"I've seen him!"

"I'm sorry?"

"Hebbel! Look, I'm not sure, but it could be. Can you come down?"

"Tempy? Is that you?"

"Who the hell do you think? Listen, Billy. I'm in town. I came down early, thought I'd do a bit of business before Saturday. Well, I was wandering along Regent Street about tea-time when I saw him, just a glimpse, reflected in a shop window. I tell you, I nearly shit myself. *Christ! Hebbel!* I thought. It was just something about the way he moved, the angle of his head. For a second I was dead certain, but when I got a good look at the fellow . . . look, Billy, can you get down tomorrow?"

"I don't know. I mean . . . Hebbel! In London? It doesn't make sense."

"Sense or not, I can't rest till I know. You'd be coming down for the reunion on Saturday anyway, wouldn't you? What's two days?"

"I suppose I could. But . . . look, Tempy, what do you want me to do?"

"Just take a look at him. I followed him. He's staying at the Kirriemuir Hotel. Listen, where do you get your train from? Leeds, isn't it? OK. I'll be at Kings Cross to meet the first train from Leeds after ten o'clock."

And that had been that. Goldsmith had phoned Timkins, the manager of the car-hire firm for which he worked, and had met with no opposition to his request for two days off. The end of September was a rela-tively slack period. But in any case, he was deter-

mined to go. He had spent a restless night, his brief
moments of sleep full of marching feet and the chatter
of machine-gun fire, and by the time he reached London the following day, he had been ready to
see Templewood accompanied by Sturmbannführer
Nikolaus Hebbel resplendent in full SS uniform.

Instead they had to wait until evening.

And for *this*!

"What made you ring?" He had to repeat the question.

Templewood looked very tired. There had been an
aura of nervous excitement about him all day, but now
it had died and he sat like a spent runner. A loser.

"I was just so certain," he answered. "On the phone
I said I wasn't, but I was. I followed him back here,
right up to his room. Then I managed to check with
the book. He's registered as Neil Housman. The same
initials. That seemed to clinch it. I was hoping you'd
take one look and say, *that's him*! But you didn't.
Looking at him now, I don't blame you! Christ, it's
probably just the reunion being so near. You know
how your mind starts going back over things. Perhaps
I'm just a bit obsessed."

He laughed, not very successfully.

Goldsmith shook his head wonderingly.

"Here in London! I mean, Buenos Aires perhaps;
but London!"

"I worked it all out. It seemed so obvious. If I were
a bright SS Major, what would I do when I saw how
the war was going? Not quite powerful enough or
influential enough to have the aeroplane or the sub-
marine booked for South America, I might just pick
on some enemy POW with the same physical charac-
teristics and no close next-of-kin and get myself con-
veyed to the last country on earth anyone would be
looking for me. A bit of loot stashed away in a nice
German cave ready to be picked up on my continental
holiday a few years after the war ended. It makes a
good story, you must admit. But hell, looking at him
now, I just don't know."

They stared through the glass doorway into the bar.

The man called Housman was talking with the barman, waving his left hand to emphasize some point.

"I'm sorry about this, Billy," said Templewood.
"Come on. I'll buy you a dinner to compensate."

"Hold on a second," said Goldsmith. Strangely,
now that Templewood seemed willing to concede that
he had made an absurd mistake, Goldsmith found
himself looking much more critically at Housman, no
longer just contrasting him with the uniformed figure
of twenty years earlier, but now trying to fill that
figure out, give it a moustache, lengthen and grizzle its
hair. That gesture with the left hand . . . how accurate
could memory be? The things we imagine we remember best are those we bring to mind most frequently
and are therefore most likely to have embellished or
embroidered.

Housman picked up his glass in his left hand and
finished his sherry. With a cheerful wave to the barman, he rose from his stool and made for the door.

"Hebbel was left-handed," said Goldsmith. It was
half a question.

"Was he?" Templewood examined his own hands as
an *aide-memoire*. The top knuckle of the middle finger
on his right hand was missing, a deformity which he
assured his friends had unimaginable erotic advan-
tages. *When he's ninety*, someone in the barracks had
said with envious admiration, *Tempy will use his
crutches*.

"Yes, I think he was." He sounded unimpressed.
"Shall we move?"

Housman came out of the bar and headed for the
toilet.

"I won't be a sec," said Goldsmith. He rose and
followed Housman.

The bright strip-lighting glinted back from sea-green
tiles. He stood a polite distance from Housman and
pretended to urinate. It was difficult to take a close
look at the man in such a position without drawing
attention to himself, and he had the old working-class
fear of being thought queer. But when Housman filled
a wash-basin and began meticulously to cleanse his

hands, it was possible to examine him fairly closely through the mirror.

He had a long, strong-boned face, good very white teeth and his eyes were dark-blue almost to blackness. Nothing there which helped one way or another. The general structure matched Hebbel's, but then, thought Goldsmith looking at his own deep-lined wind-and-sun-tanned face, so does mine. Housman's teeth he suspected were expensively false, which would be the kind of efficient disposal of a possible source of identification he would expect from Hebbel. The eyes were a darker blue than he recalled. But memory could deceive. Or such things might change. Or nowadays you could get tinted contact lenses if you had the money to pay.

Housman did not look as if he were short of cash. His clothes were elegantly cut and the gold wristwatch and signet ring he had removed while washing his hands looked as if they had cost a couple of months of Goldsmith's salary.

It was the man's hands which Goldsmith now focused on. He watched them intertwining, flexing, rubbing together under the hot-air dryer. The noise from the machine was a deep and somehow disturbing hum. It was like (or was his mind again creating memories?) the noise from the generator plant which day and night seemed to fill the air of the Waffen SS camp near the Normandy village of Anet. As he watched the man's hands rubbing together, the noise seemed to fill his mind and set his whole body vibrating in harmony.

Suddenly it stopped. The silence left Goldsmith almost paralysed. Housman turned, picked up his watch and ring and put them on. He nodded at Goldsmith, moved away, paused uncertainly and said, "Are you all right?"

The voice had a strangely husky timbre, as though a second rate impressionist was "doing" Paul Robeson.

"Yes, thanks. Fine," said Goldsmith brusquely.

"Good," said Housman with a smile and left.

A few moments later Goldsmith rejoined Templewood.

"Where did he go?"

"In to dinner. Us too, I think. But not here. I've
found a rather nice little *trattoria* in Dean Street. That
suit you?"

"If you like," said Goldsmith shortly. He was usually amused by the veneer of urbanity his companion
had collected since the war. Tonight it seemed shod-
dily pretentious.

The walk through the night air improved his spirits,
and as he listened to Templewood ordering their meal
with serious expertise, he was able to be amused once
more. Did this new sophistication of technique mean
that Templewood's powers had improved or declined
since the days when he claimed that if he couldn't
have a girl up against a wall in ten minutes, she was no
use to him?

"Now, for *antipasto*, how does *funghi acciugati al
forno* grab you?"

"Come on, Tempy. You're not seducing me. Prac-
tise in your own time."

"But I *am* paying," protested Templewood humor-
ously.

"In that case I'll have another scotch."

The waiter left and the two men sipped their drinks.

"Well?" said Templewood finally.

"What?"

"You've been gnawing away at something since we
left the hotel. Spit it out."

"It's most unlikely that he's Hebbel."

"All right. I agree. I've said I'm sorry."

"But it'd be silly not to make sure."

Templewood was re-arranging the cutlery on the table top like a retired general demonstrating strategy.

"You think you spotted a resemblance too?" he
asked quietly.

"I'm very suggestible. That's why I'm going to be
eating chunks of soft plastic with Technicolour sauce in

a moment. No. I didn't spot a resemblance. But I watched his hands and I felt frightened."

"That's what I felt when I first spotted him in Regent Street," said Templewood excitedly. "But it's not much."

"No. He spoke to me in the bog."

"You took a chance, didn't you?"

"What of? Like you say, I've changed beyond recognition. But his voice was interesting."

"You recognized it?" asked Templewood, raising his heavy eyebrows.

"Of course not. It was just that he sounded as if he had laryngitis, that's all."

"And what *do* you think Hebbel would sound like after eighteen years in England?" asked Templewood.

The waiter appeared with plates of what looked like toadstool caps crossed by snail spoors. He rearranged the cutlery dramatically and left.

"Suppose the million-to-one chance came off," said Goldsmith abruptly. "What then?"

"It'd be our duty to turn him in," said Templewood with a humourless smile. "Let the law take its course. He'd probably get five or six years."

He turned over one of the hemispheres on his plate. It smelt quite appetizing.

"They don't seem so keen on killing people nowadays," he continued. "It's against the trend. We might have to make a minority report."

"How do we start checking?" said Goldsmith.

"I got his address from the register," said Templewood, suddenly businesslike. "He lives up in your part of the world, just outside Sheffield. One of us had better do some checking there. I mean, if the place is full of his childhood friends, then we can pull down the shutters straightaway. Shall I look after that? I've got the car with me and I can drive there tomorrow, get back for the reunion on Saturday night. OK?"

"Fine. Shouldn't I come with you? Two of us could cover the ground much quicker. And I've got the accent."

Templewood thought for a moment.

"No. It'd be better to keep an eye on him here too. See what he gets up to, what his business is."

"Things haven't changed," said Goldsmith ironically. "You on the truck, me marching along the roadway with my knapsack on my back."

"You got the medal," said Templewood. "And if it turns out to be Hebbel, I'll let you slide the first knife in. Now eat your food and don't leave any crusts, there's a good boy."

# CHAPTER II

FRIDAY MORNING started with farce.

Housman came out of the Kirriemuir at nine-thirty sharp. He was wearing a dark brown suit and carrying a document case.

Goldsmith felt absurdly conspicuous lurking in the doorway of a block of flats opposite the hotel. The temptation he found was to ham it up, to play the part of the private eye in an old American movie. He had been there for an hour and a half, his head swathed in a morning paper, smoking cigarette after cigarette.

Now he folded the paper under his arm, ground his last cigarette beneath his heel and prepared for action.

Across the street Housman stepped into a taxi. Twenty seconds later it was out of sight.

Goldsmith had wondered if this might happen, had been unable to think of any way of counteracting it and was now left stranded with nowhere to go. Except the hotel.

He walked swiftly up to the desk.

"Mr. Housman, please."

"I'm afraid he's just left, sir," said the receptionist.

"Damn. Look, did he say where he was going? It's important."

"No, I'm sorry. Hold on a minute, though."

She went through into the small room behind the desk which housed the hotel exchange and returned with a note-pad.

"He left a number he can be reached at this morning in case there were any calls for him here."

"May I?" said Goldsmith, taking the pad. Quickly

he jotted down the number. There was a public telephone cubicle opposite the desk and he went into this
and dialed.

"Amberson and Lockhart, can I help you?" said a
woman's voice.

"Sorry. I must have the wrong number," said Goldsmith. He replaced the receiver, picked up the first
volume of the telephone directory and thumbed through
the pages. Amberson and Lockhart turned out to be
merchant bankers with an address his London A to Z
told him was just off Moorgate in the City.

He made his way there by tube. There was no
reason to hurry. It seemed unlikely that Housman was
just paying a brief visit to the bank. His deduction
turned out to be all too true and even his dawdling
journey there did not prevent him from having to hang
about for over two hours before he saw his man again.
Fortunately it was a fine warm September day, but
Goldsmith had long decided that the profession of
detective was grossly over-glamourized when Housman finally emerged. He looked relieved to be out in
the fresh air and headed west on foot. His destination
was a small very unpretentious restaurant. Goldsmith
peered through the door as though looking for somebody and saw Housman shaking hands with a thin
bald-headed man already seated at a table. The place
was quite full, but they looked settled, so Goldsmith
decided to abandon his quarry for half an hour while
he too got something to eat in a nearby pub. He
thought of abandoning the chase permanently, but
one-thirty saw him hanging around once more, waiting
for Housman to reappear. After lunch the two men
shook hands on the pavement and separated. Housman looked very pleased with himself and walked with
the bouncy step of one who has put work behind him
and now anticipates the rewards of pleasure. He strode
smartly along Moorgate to Finsbury Square, where he
turned off the main thoroughfare and at the same
brisk pace made his way along streets whose names
Goldsmith did not know. He began to fear that he had
been spotted and that his quarry was merely testing

him. At the same time the absurdity of his situation
struck him. How could he explain following a complete stranger for miles through the streets of London?
Perhaps Housman would recall their encounter in the
hotel loo the previous evening. He dropped back to a
distance of more than a hundred yards. Ahead, Housman turned right and Goldsmith accelerated once more,
but when he reached the corner, the man had disappeared.

It was a long street, too long, he decided, for Housman to have turned another corner. It meant he must
be in one of the buildings, but short of knocking on
every door, there was no way of discovering which.

The street was called Wath Grove, though whatever
trees had once flourished there must by now have
been well on their way to coal. It looked as if it might
once have been fashionable and perhaps the pendulum
was swinging back once more. Several of the Victorian
terraced houses bore signs of refurbishing, and decorators had erected their scaffolding outside a couple of
others.

Goldsmith measured the maximum distance Housman could have covered before turning off and added
another twenty yards. Unless he had broken into a run
he must be in one of these houses. If he *had* broken
into a run, it could only be because he knew he was
being followed and Goldsmith discounted this. An
innocent man was not going to take to his heels in
broad daylight in London. And Hebbel would have
the behaviour of the innocent perfectly worked out.

But it couldn't be Hebbel. There was no chance,
Goldsmith assured himself. He and Templewood were
like children who have been chased by a fierce dog
and see its lineaments in all animals thereafter. No,
that exaggerated the position. He hadn't given Hebbel
a thought since the last reunion. In fact nowadays it
was only these reunions which ever brought the man
to mind. He ought to stop going, had even been thinking about it this year, but had been told it helped his
political image. He wondered what being arrested for
loitering would do to the image. And did he care?

He had over an hour to occupy himself with such gloomy thoughts, and by the end of that time he was so totally immersed in his self-examination that he almost missed Housman's reappearance. A workman on one of the sets of scaffolding dropped a brush and shouted a warning. Housman, who had just come down the steps of the house next door, ducked instinctively though he was well clear of risk, and Goldsmith, his attention drawn by the shout, saw him wave in sheepish reassurance at a face which appeared momentarily at a second-floor window.

It was now late afternoon. Housman spent the next hour wandering round the West End stores until they closed. He made a couple of purchases that Goldsmith was close enough to see; a long double string of beads, 'twenties style and very fashionable at the moment, and a bottle of perfume. Presents for the family? Goldsmith wondered. Somehow the idea that Housman might have wife and children made this whole business of shadowing him seem ludicrous and mean. He might have given it up there and then had not the memory of Housman's afternoon visit and its most obvious interpretation discredited the family-man image.

In any case the rest was easy, if dull. Housman returned to his hotel, stayed in his room until eight, had a leisurely dinner by himself, and spent an hour in the television room. About half past nine, he was called away from the television set to take a phone call. It left him looking very pensive, and after another quick drink, he went up to his room.

Goldsmith, thoroughly disenchanted with the life of a private detective, returned to his own hotel to find the bar had closed. Fortunately he had a bottle of scotch in his case and two or three stiff nips of this helped to drive out some of the day's cold and disillusion. But he fell asleep, resolved that the following morning as far as he was concerned Housman could rape the Lord Mayor and rob the Bank of England completely unobserved.

He woke up quite early wondering what Housman

could be going to do on a Saturday in London if he didn't go home. Another visit to Wath Grove perhaps? Or perhaps it was to be a day of work; if you wanted to be really rich or really powerful you ignored weekends. Which will I become? he wondered, thinking that this was the first Saturday in months he himself had not woken to a list of engagements. In local government, an unmarried councillor, living alone, was an obvious target when others pleaded the sanctity of familial togetherness. Not that it hadn't worked for him as well. It had got him noticed, got him known. Got him on the short list. But that was nothing. You hung on by your fingertips and it didn't take much agitation to shake you off.

He groaned and began to get up. This Housman business was a complete waste of time, he was convinced. A childish nightmare; the last ravings of a past that should have been allowed to die years earlier. But he had to do his part. He couldn't afford to leave it to Templewood. There was a streak of wildness in the man which needed outside control. Left to himself, he was quite capable of acting on the flimsiest evidence and stirring up a public furore. His apparent willingness to let things drop on Thursday evening had clearly been a transient thing. Goldsmith wondered how he was getting on in Sheffield and prayed he was treading carefully.

He went downstairs to breakfast, stopping first at the desk to inquire if there were any nearby car-hire firms they could recommend, smiling politely as the receptionist confided in him that most hire businesses were run by crooks. This morning he was determined that he was not going to be left afoot while Housman disappeared in a taxi. Nor was he going to be standing around on street corners while his man was indoors in warmth and comfort.

This morning Housman walked.

Goldsmith, who had already discovered the inconveniences of double-parking outside the Kirriemuir, now experienced the greater difficulties of stalking a pedestrian in a car.

He crawled along in bottom gear for a while. Next he tried stopping till Housman got a good distance ahead, driving after him at near normal speed, and stopping once more. Both methods attracted the disapproval of other road-users, and he was heartily glad when Housman went into a large office block near Holborn.

Parking again presented a problem, but he discovered it was possible to make a circuit of the block in under a minute which kept the odds on missing Housman very low. The man reappeared after an hour, glanced at his watch and set off walking once more in the direction of Covent Garden. His destination was a pub near Bow Street and this time Goldsmith was in luck, a parking meter bay becoming vacant just as he drew level with the pub.

Inside, Housman was sitting with two other men, one about fifty, the other much younger. They were obviously old acquaintances and the conversation was lively and relaxed. After a couple of drinks they went to the lunch counter and selected generous portions of shepherd's pie. Goldsmith followed suit.

At half past one, the younger man left and the other two talked more confidentially for a while. Then about half an hour later they too rose and the chase was on once more.

Outside, Goldsmith found he had a parking ticket. He had simply forgotten about the car and he felt disproportionately indignant. But his spirits rose again when he saw the two men climb into a black Mercedes (which seemed singularly free of any parking ticket) and drive away together.

Where now? he wondered, for the first time feeling the excitement of pursuit. His mind threw up any number of exotic possibilities which did not include Highbury where Arsenal were playing Manchester United. Housman and his companion bought tickets and went into the ground. Goldsmith could whip up no enthusiasm for the encounter and suddenly it all seemed very pointless. He did not wait, but drove back to his hotel to see if Templewood had returned

yet. There was no sign of him, nor any message, and
he went up to his room, threw himself on the bed and
lay there, staring at the ceiling for some time. Finally
just when he had decided this was a futile pastime and
there must be more profitable ways of employing the
afternoon, he fell asleep.

# CHAPTER III

HE SLEPT so well that he was late for the reunion and most of the others had two or three drinks' start on him. The noise as he entered the packed room was tremendous. The impression of overcrowding was only relative, however. Up till five years earlier, they had used the Banqueting Suite on the floor above, but finally it had begun to look like a rugby pitch in a seven-a-side match, all space and no players. Now they took one of the small reception rooms; eventually a single bedroom would probably be enough, thought Goldsmith cynically.

He was one of the youngest there. Called up early in '44, he had completed his training and joined the regiment just a few weeks before D-Day. And as he and most of the rest of his platoon had been captured within hours of the first landings, his claims to have taken part in the war were to some extent fraudulent. Yet he was a minor regimental hero. Lieutenant (now Colonel) Maxwell, his platoon commander, left for dead by the Germans, had described Goldsmith's conduct under fire in such terms that when he was liberated in 1945, he discovered he had been awarded the DCM. Templewood, the only other surviving member of the captured platoon, had found this a great source of satire. Only a year older, he sometimes talked as if he had fought on every front since 1939.

There was no sign of him in the room now and others were claiming Goldsmith's attention. He found himself drawn into a group which included Maxwell, a short ugly man in his mid-forties.

"You well, Goldsmith? You're late. Get him a drink somebody; get him a couple; we want no malingerers tonight!"

He always put on a special voice and manner for these affairs, half parodying the traditional old-style army officer. But Goldsmith knew him as an astute and sensitive man. His injuries had kept him out of the fighting for the rest of the war, but he had been posted to the staff of an Intelligence Corps Field Security Section in 1945 and later became attached to the Allied War Crimes Commission.

After Goldsmith and Templewood had been released from their confinement it was Maxwell who had sought them out to question them about Hebbel. Evidence against the SS man had already begun to accumulate from French Resistance sources, according to which he had ruthlessly and on occasion personally disposed of hostages taken in reprisal against Resistance activities. But it was the disappearance of seven members of his old platoon which particularly concerned Maxwell.

Goldsmith and Templewood had been able to confirm the fragmented version of the French locals. They had been subjected to intensive interrogation about the Allied landings till finally, partly *pour encourager les autres*, partly because his unit might have to move fast and Hebbel did not want to be encumbered with prisoners, but mainly, Templewood suggested, for kicks, the killing started.

An air attack had given them the chance to escape. There was no hope of getting back to the Allied lines, but at least they had been able to get themselves recaptured by a normal Wehrmacht unit who had shipped them back to Germany for the rest of the war.

After the war Hebbel had disappeared without trace. At first when the reunions started in 1947, Maxwell had kept Goldsmith and Templewood abreast of the search. Their evidence had been carefully recorded and they would be two of the principal prosecution witnesses if and when the man was caught.

But the trail had long been cold and time dulls even the sharpest memories, and it was many years now since Hebbel had been mentioned to Goldsmith by anyone other than Templewood. So it was like having his thoughts spoken aloud when suddenly under cover of a raucous outburst of laughter at some remembered privation, Maxwell said to him, "By the way, bit of news that might interest. Your friend Hebbel. Strange after all this time, but there may be a line."

"You mean, they know where he is?" demanded Goldsmith. What the news would mean to him, he was no longer sure.

"Not exactly. No, thing was, it seems, that the Israelis crossed his trail when they were digging out Eichmann in 1960. They're not much worried themselves, bigger fish, and Hebbel was never firmly linked with any Final Solution stuff. No, he's one for us. But there's a lot of mutual back-scratching goes on, you understand. So, well, Peru. That's where the line led. Safe there, of course. At least with our methods. Someone went in to check, of course. Good to be certain."

"And did they find him?" asked Goldsmith.

"No. Not a sign." Maxwell laughed, or rather made a sound which was close to a laugh in everything except humour. "No. But after Eichmann, they'd all bury themselves a bit deeper, eh? Let's get another drink. Tell me about yourself. How's the politics? See you're trying for the big time, eh?"

"Yes," said Goldsmith, deciding suddenly that he was relieved. Hebbel safely in Peru took the burden of decision from his shoulders. The Nazi wasn't going to leave his bolthole in a hurry and he, Goldsmith, felt no compulsion to go after him there with an assassin's knife. Even Templewood would be daunted by such a prospect.

"And just how big is the big time?"

It was Templewood, immaculate in a dinner jacket, frilled dress shirt and regimental cummerbund.

"There you are," said Maxwell. "Have a drink. Goldsmith's to be an MP, that's how big."

"You never told me about that, Billy," accused Templewood.

"It's an anticipation," said Goldsmith. "I'm just on the candidate short list, that's all. I'm not even sure how the Colonel knows?"

"Such things are noticed," said Maxwell mysteriously. "Good intelligence, that's the thing. I like to keep a check. Excuse me now, there's Sergeant-Major Gilbert. Owed me a pound for twenty-two years."

"Stupid sod," grunted Templewood as they watched him go.

"You think so?"

"He's still in the bloody army, isn't he? So you're headed for Parliament, Billy. Well, well. You'll have to watch your step then, won't want to risk getting your feet wet."

"It's a long road yet," said Goldsmith, Maxwell's new information permitting him to take the gibe equably. Briefly he passed it on.

"Peru," repeated Templewood thoughtfully. "That always seemed the best bet, of course."

"Do you want him badly enough to go to Peru?" asked Goldsmith, half mocking.

"Evidently you don't. Well, if that's the case, I've been wasting my time these past two days. We'd better get stuck into the booze before these sods drink the place dry."

The catering was informal, a buffet and a bar, to permit greater freedom of movement and opportunity of renewing old acquaintance. There would be a couple of speeches midway through the evening, but nothing more structured than that. If you had to have these things, thought Goldsmith, this was at least a bearable way to do it.

He fought his way back from the buffet with two crowded plates while Templewood refilled their glasses.

"No food for me, thanks."

"Lost your appetite?"

"For this stuff, yes. They must bring it down from Catterick in bins. Anyway, I've got something lined up for later. A bite of supper, then a big helping of the old Eve's pudding for afters. Half an hour of this lot'll do me."

"I don't know why you bother to come," observed Goldsmith.

"Me neither."

Goldsmith put the plates down on a small table already overcrowded with glasses and a malodorous ash-tray. He took his drink from Templewood and sipped it reflectively.

"What did you get up to then?" asked Templewood.

"Me? Oh, I nearly went to see Arsenal play, but I couldn't face it," he said with a laugh. "It was a complete waste of time. You?"

"Almost as bad. I saw a lot of Sheffield. Friend Housman is well known there. Has a lot of money; big house; belongs to the Rotary Club, Conservative Association, Masons. You name it."

"He's not a churchwarden and a magistrate as well, is he?" asked Goldsmith.

"Could be."

"Where does the money come from. Wealthy family?"

"No," said Templewood thoughtfully. "No family background at all, not locally. Apart from his own immediate family, I mean. Wife and one kid. She's local, was his secretary. I was able to get quite a lot on his business background. My company do a lot of business round there so I've got contacts."

Templewood was Sales Manager of Domicol, the country's fourth largest manufacturers of decorators' supplies, or so their publicity said (fourth in size but first in service). His years in the sales field had provided him with a bottomless sack of commercial travellers' stories, all based (or so he claimed) on his own experience.

"He's a partner in J. T. Hardy's, the development company. We've sold them a lot of stuff in our time, but I've never come across Housman. Those who know say he's the driving force there, but likes to keep in the background."

"Yes," interrupted Goldsmith. "And he doesn't exactly splash his money around when he's in London, does he? The Kirriemuir's all right, but it's not the Savoy. Or even the Hilton."

"Perhaps it's just his business method. It certainly works. When Housman turned up in the early 'fifties, J. T. Hardy's was a small family building firm. He bought in, started things moving, and a few years ago they stopped being builders and became developers."

"I know the name," said Goldsmith. "They've used our firm sometimes to pick up people at the Leeds/Bradford airport."

"Have they?" said Templewood without interest. "Must be rich for your prices."

They refilled their glasses and stood without speaking for a moment, listening to the ebb and flow of military nostalgia all around them.

Goldsmith spoke reflectively.

"Didn't Maxwell once tell us that Hebbel was training as an architect before the war, prior to joining his family's civil engineering business?"

"Did he? So what? I suppose everybody was going to do something else before the war. Me, I might have become a monk!"

Templewood laughed raucously at the thought and Goldsmith began to feel angry.

"So you admit now it was just a farce? Listen, Tempy, I'm a busy man, I don't like wasting a couple of days chasing shadows."

"You're a politician, Billy," said Templewood lightly. "I thought you'd have been used to it."

"Oh, go to hell! You're the most self-centered bastard I know."

He turned away, but Templewood grasped his arm.

"Look, Billy, I'm sorry. I'm not doing the big kiss-your-arse apology thing, because I've still got a feeling about this boy. But that's all. Just let's stand back from it awhile. I'll keep sniffing around now I know where to sniff, and you get back to waving the people's flag. OK?"

Someone somewhere was banging a glass on a table. Templewood looked round in alarm. "Oh Christ!" he said. "It sounds like speech time. I'm off. Nice to see you again. Next year, eh? DV and WP. Sorry to have mucked your week up."

"Hold on," said Goldsmith, suddenly full of guilt at his outburst. A few drinks quickly brought out a latent sentimental vein in him. Templewood might be an egotistical sexual obsessive who fancied himself as a detective, but there were strong bonds of experience holding them together.

"Have another drink before you go."

"Can't, old son. Don't want the lady to start without me, do I?"

"Then give me a ring tomorrow morning. I needn't catch a train till mid-afternoon. We could lunch together."

"OK. I won't promise, depends on how many encores I take. But I'll try. See you!"

He moved away with his characteristic confident strut; like a bantam heading for the hen-coop, thought Goldsmith.

"Billy? Billy Goldsmith!" said a voice behind him. "How's tricks? For God's sake, get that glass filled!"

He turned, only half recognized the man who so familiarly greeted him, but gladly accepted the invitation to fill his glass.

Goldsmith usually stayed sober, even on occasions like this. There were gaps in himself whose emptiness sometimes ached, but he had never found alcohol could even begin to fill them. And he was not a man who readily slackened his lines of control. But tonight he gave himself over entirely to the spirit of nostalgic euphoria which ruled the reunion. The drink took a rapid hold on his unaccustomed senses and at ten o'clock, after three or four madly swaying choruses of "Bless 'em All," he found himself kneeling over a pink marble lavatory bowl wondering whether to be sick or not.

Behind him perched on the edge of a huge bath was Colonel Maxwell.

"Vitreous China," read Goldsmith, piecing together the letters on the marble. "Like perfidious Albion. All Chinese are vitreous."

"Made your mind up yet?" demanded Maxwell.

Goldsmith examined himself mentally, then stood up and looked at himself in the mirror. His reflection stared solemnly back. Even drunk, it was a face which promised control, discretion, reliability. If Maxwell had not been there, he might have spat right into it.

"I think I'll be all right," he said.

"Right. Try the cold water," said Maxwell.

Obediently he bent his head down into the hand basin and ran the cold tap, cupping his hands and splashing the icy stream into his face.

"That's enough," commanded Maxwell. "Fresh air, a stiff walk, that'll do the trick."

Minutes later they were strolling along Regent Street together.

"No need for you to come," protested Goldsmith.

"That's all right. I need the walk. Can't take the stuff like I used to."

"I wouldn't have noticed," answered Goldsmith.

"No? Well, you don't show much yourself either. Not till you start falling over."

They continued in silence for a while. The traffic was heavy and the pavements fairly crowded. It was a relief when Maxwell, very much in control, turned right and led him into a comparatively quiet maze of streets which took them into Soho.

"Interested in this stuff?" asked Maxwell with a short wave of the hand.

Goldsmith wasn't certain whether he meant Greek food or naked Ceylonese snake-dancers.

"No," he said, inclusively.

"More Templewood's style, eh? He left early."

"He'd be flattered you noticed."

"I doubt it. Interesting fellow, in some ways. Seems to be doing all right. You see a lot of him?"

"No. Once a year at the reunion and that's about it."

"I see. Not married, is he?"

"No. On the contrary," Goldsmith laughed.

"Queer, you mean?"

"No! Just very hetero-hetero."

"Oh. And you?"

Again he wasn't sure of the precise direction of Maxwell's question.

"No." The inclusive negative seemed to be in order once more.

"I thought these political fellows—selection boards, that sort of thing—liked safe family men?"

"Often they do. Which might be why I won't get selected."

"I think you'll get anything you like, Goldsmith," said Maxwell. "Feeling OK now? See you next year then. Good luck."

It was an abrupt leave-taking and Goldsmith was left standing on the pavement, staring after the Colonel's stocky erect figure as he marched briskly back the way they had come.

"Continuous show, friend," said a club tout from a nearby doorway, mistaking his hesitation. "Leaves nothing to the imagination. If you can imagine it, we can show it."

"I doubt it," said Goldsmith and continued on his way. His nerves and muscles seemed to be overcharged, sending little shock waves of energy rippling through his body so that he had to increase his pace to absorb them. The thought of going to bed, or even of sitting down, had no appeal at all. He had felt like this before and knew that a night of pure white insomnia lay ahead unless he could push himself into exhaustion.

His rapid stride had taken him across Charing Cross Road and he bore right now making up to New Oxford Street. Another few minutes could bring him to the Kirriemuir Hotel, he realized. A pity it was not earlier. He felt much more in the mood for tailing Housman now than he had hitherto.

His mind began to turn over what Templewood had told him at the reunion. The information about Housman's business background fitted with the visits he had made in the past couple of days. Except, of course, to the house in Wath Grove.

He began to picture Housman in his mind and for some reason the image he got was more like Hebbel than ever before. It was the drink, of course. Hebbel

was in Peru. Or dead perhaps. One of the tens of
thousands over whose anonymous bones the new cities
of Germany's economic miracle had arisen. Hebbel
could not possibly be Housman, respectable Rotarian
Housman, living in some provincial stockbroker belt
with his wife and 2.4 children. Was he married? He
tried to recall if Templewood had said. Probably he
was. Probably he had married his childhood sweet-
heart, courted long years since in the streets of . . .
why not Manchester? There had to be some reason for
his choice of football match that afternoon.

Yes, probably a few words with his wife and family
would have clarified matters in a trice. He sounded a
reserved kind of man, not the type who would reveal
everything about himself to mere business acquaintances.

Yet he had not looked like a naturally reserved kind
of man sitting at the bar chatting to the barman; nor
when he had inquired if Goldsmith were ill in the
washroom.

There was a bit of mystery about him. Goldsmith
doubted very much if it was his own particular mystery, but it certainly existed.

His rapid pace and deep introspection finally brought
about what it had been threatening for several minutes. He collided heavily with someone and they clung
to each other for support and recovery.

"I'm sorry," said Goldsmith breathlessly.

"You bloody well should be," snapped the man he
had collided with. He was a balding, horsy-faced man
with a Yorkshire accent and a bad-tempered expres-
sion. An angry Yorkshireman was not something
Goldsmith particularly wanted at the moment. As a
councillor, half his life seemed to be spent dealing
with angry Yorkshiremen. He smiled conciliatingly,
then turned to get his bearings.

He accepted as part of life's fateful pattern the fact
that he was at the foot of the steps which led up to the
Kirriemuir Hotel. And it needed no conscious effort
of will to set him walking up the steps.

# CHAPTER IV

THE ONLY OCCUPANTS of the entrance lounge were two middle-aged women, sitting in the chairs he and Templewood had used two nights earlier. They were discussing a disappointingly immoral play they had just seen. Schoolteachers, on a cultural weekend, Goldsmith categorized them in passing.

The reception desk was empty. He spun the open registration book round, flipped back a page and spotted Housman's name instantly, Room 26. He looked at the key-board. The 26 peg was empty. Housman must be in his room, or else in the bar or TV lounge with the key in his pocket.

Goldsmith was normally a most circumspect man, but from time to time he found himself started on a course of action which he felt compelled to pursue, no matter what areas of irrationality and rashness lay ahead. Perhaps his awareness of this daemonic urge was the reason for his normal circumspection. He began to climb the stairs now, having no idea what he was going to do or say when he reached Housman's room, but equally bereft of the power to halt himself.

Room 26 was on the second floor at the back of the hotel, far from the best room even in this very modest establishment. He wondered once again at Housman's reluctance to live in the luxury which it seemed he could afford.

There was no reply to his knock. He tried a second time with the same result and finally turned the handle. The door swung open with a faint creak.

A bedside lamp was on, but the room was empty.

The key lay on the dressing-table. His second guess was right; Housman must have gone out briefly, for a nightcap perhaps or to catch the late news. This was not the kind of hotel which piped television to all its guests. That at least was in its favour, as were the room's dimensions. A more recent building would have carved the space used here into three or even four aseptic catafalques in which a man could feel he had taken one step towards the tomb. But here it was possible, if you desired, to take a turn round the bed before getting into it.

Goldsmith found he had entered and closed the door behind him. There was no point in hesitating now. Delay only increased the chances of being caught. What had promised to be an embarrassing confrontation had turned into a criminal act and generally the only trick to criminal success is speed.

He began to search.

Beside the wardrobe was an old brown leather suitcase which contained a plastic bag full of discarded clothing. The wardrobe itself held the light grey suit he had seen Housman wearing and another more formal dark grey suit. On the dressing-table was a small framed snapshot of a family group, Housman and, presumably, his wife and daughter. They looked well together. The dressing-table drawers revealed nothing out of the ordinary; handkerchiefs, underclothes, toilet articles.

What the hell do I expect? Goldsmith asked himself savagely. Swastikas? The daemon was weakening and he was becoming more and more aware of the absurdity of his situation.

Behind him something moved. He almost fell as he turned in panic. The full-length curtains were billowing towards him as a sudden breeze puffed in through the wide open sash-window. He let out a long breath of relief which felt as strong as the breeze itself, went to the window to close it, then checked himself, realizing what a giveaway it would be. He leaned on the low sill and peered out. It was not a pleasant prospect; below, there was a fifty-foot drop into a paved kitchen area, littered with boxes, bins and crates, and on all sides loomed the shadowy outlines of buildings, irregularly patterned with squares and rectangles of vinegary light. The thought of the many miles in each direction covered by bricks and mortar suddenly pressed in hard on his mind and he closed his eyes. He hated any sense of confinement and had steadfastly resisted the efforts of the local Labour Party to persuade him to leave his stone-built cottage on the fringe of the Dales and move back into the heart of the ward for which he was councillor.

The breeze dropped, the curtains fell back, he opened his eyes. And found himself looking down at the black leather and chrome document case he had seen Housman carrying. He picked it up, placed it on the bed and tried the catch. It was locked. By now the daemon was quite exhausted and the inexorable pressures which had brought him to the room were being replaced by the more erratic forces of panic. He abandoned the case and headed for the door, but his eyes fell on a pile of loose change and a bunch of keys by the bedside lamp. He paused, indecisive. What could the case hold which could help him in any way? What did *help* mean in this situation?

Angrily he snatched up the keys and at his first attempt selected the one which fitted the lock.

Unsurprisingly it was full of documents. They were financial, legal, incomprehensible at such a short viewing, but all relating to J. T. Hardy's. Some large development project seemed to be in the offing and Amberson and Lockhart's were involved in backing it. It all fitted in with Housman's movements.

In a pocket in the lid of the case he found some letters, again all obviously connected with business except one, the envelope of which was handwritten. Goldsmith was feeling ashamed of himself now and hesitated about reading it. There was something else in the pocket, in a square buff envelope. He postponed his decision about the letter, thrusting it into his own pocket while he shook out the contents of this envelope.

On to the pale green bedspread fell a passport. Quietly he opened it. Housman's face, slightly younger, stared out at him. He glanced at the date of issue, 1954, then turned back to the face. The moustache, the spectacles, how much could they change a man? And what was he comparing it with anyway? A chimera, bred of fancy out of fear.

The page opposite the photograph was more helpful. Profession—company director. Place and date of birth—Sunderland 11.11.18. A present for Armistice Day. Residence—England. Height—5′11″. Colour of eyes—blue. Colour of hair—fair. Special peculiarities—none.

The details of date and place of birth at least could be checked, thought Goldsmith. He had no doubt that his research would prove that a child called Neil Housman had been born on that day, and very little that this face belonged to that child. It was time to go. He had lingered too long already and to be caught now with the document case open on the bed would be impossible to explain. He replaced the documents neatly, picked up the passport and its envelope, then before putting them back on an impulse he riffled through the visa pages.

Housman was a much travelled man, was his first thought. But his second thought was much more riveting, so much so that he did not hear the bedroom door open.

In April of the previous year, Housman had visited Peru. And in May two years before that.

"What the hell do you think you're doing?" The voice was distinctive.

He looked up.

Standing in the doorway, wearing a dressing-gown and pink from freshly bathing, was Housman.

Foolish of me, thought Goldsmith dispassionately. The money and the keys should have told me.

He felt surprisingly in control.

"Police," he said, not in the hope of deceiving, but merely trying to delay the other's call for assistance. It seemed to work, even though the look on Housman's face was nine parts incredulity.

"Show me your warrant card," he demanded.

"What were you doing in Peru last year?" asked Goldsmith.

"What's that got to do with you?"

Housman reached for the bedside telephone.

"I've seen you before," he continued. "In the loo the other night. You couldn't manage a piss."

"Do you want everyone to know about this stuff?" Goldsmith tapped the case. "And Wath Grove?"

Housman replaced the receiver. He looked very self-possessed.

"Jesus wept," he said. "How many of you are there?"

Goldsmith ignored this odd question, hoping that an air of confidence would indicate the place was full of his accomplices.

"I'm sure we can settle things amicably," he said. "Just tell me about Peru."

"She's barking up the wrong tree. Peru was merely business. What are you after?"

Goldsmith felt unwell. He did not like what was happening here. "She" must be Housman's wife who the man imagined had hired him. The thought of the damage he might be doing to their relationship troubled him greatly. He had no right to let his own search for Hebbel harm innocent people. Could Peru be a coincidence? It was a stupid question. Anything could be coincidence. He found that he was massaging his forehead in an effort to ease away the internal pressure building up there.

"Are you all right?" asked Housman. He might have been parodying his concern at their first brief meeting, but Goldsmith was not up to detecting such subtleties and infinitely less capable of penetrating defences which (if they existed) had been carefully built up over twenty years.

He dropped the passport into the case and set off for the door. Housman barred his way.

"Not leaving are you?"

"I'll be in touch," he managed to say.

"Oh no. We settle this now. You've been through my papers, now it's my turn to check on you."

Housman, very confident of both physical and mental dominance, took hold of Goldsmith's jacket and tried to remove his wallet. Resistance was instinctive; the thought that the hands might be Hebbel's made it violent. He brought his arms between them, flinging them wide and breaking the other's grip.

"Christ!" ejaculated Housman, staggering back and nursing his aching wrists. Goldsmith started for the door again, Housman came at him from the side and launched an attack at his head with more fury than technique. Goldsmith grabbed the loose material of his dressing-gown and tried to fling him off once more, but the other man was ready this time and countered by grasping his jacket lapels.

For a few moments they turned round and round, the only noise being involuntary grunts of effort and the slither and pad of feet as they made inexpert attempts to trip or cross-buttock each other.

All Goldsmith wanted now was to get out, not merely of the room and the hotel, but out of the whole sprawling mass of bricks and stone and stench of humanity that was London. His opponent's eyes were bright with something which might have been enjoyment of the struggle and his features were taut with the will to win. His dressing-gown belt had come undone and the garment fell away from his naked body like the skirts of a dancer in some obscene floor show. An ugly raised scar ran down from his adam's apple then turned along his collar bone. Goldsmith felt desperately sick. His need to get outside into the fresh air had left the area of mere health and entered that of survival.

A sudden change of tactics brought Housman close up against him. The man tried to use his forehead as a battering-ram and caught Goldsmith a painful blow above the right eye. In retaliation he stamped down violently on Housman's naked foot. He screamed, his grip relaxed, Goldsmith tightened his own on the dressing-gown front, did a sharp half-turn and hurled the man from him with all his strength.

He was propelled across the room out of control

straight towards the curtained window. The lower sill caught him behind the knees; involuntarily he sat down; the curtains parted behind him.

Then he was gone.

It was so stagy that Goldsmith could not take it in for a moment. Even when he parted the curtains and peered down into the dimly lit kitchen area below, the body had that carefully arranged look the cinema always produces in such vertical shots.

A door was opening below. Someone had heard the noise of the fall or perhaps was just coming out to deposit rubbish in a bin. The panel of light fell directly across Housman's body.

Goldsmith waited no longer. He hoped that he would have gone down himself to see how badly injured the man was. But now the need was removed and only the need for flight remained. He felt quite cool.

He glanced quickly round the room. It bore surprisingly little evidence of struggle. The epic qualities of the fight had been mainly subjective. A rug needed straightening. He closed the document case and placed it by the bed.

The corridor outside was empty. He ran down the stairs, checked at the bottom, saw that the lounge still contained only the two culture-seeking teachers, walked swiftly by them and out into the night.

It was not till he reached his own hotel room that he realized his coolness had not extended to checking his own appearance. His clothes were disheveled, one of his lapels was torn, and he had an angry contusion over his right eye.

He sat on the bed and poured himself a whisky. He felt he needed it badly, but one sip was enough to undo all Colonel Maxwell's earlier good work and he was violently and comprehensively sick.

# CHAPTER V

HE WAS AWOKEN by bells and found himself sprawled stiff and still fully clothed on top of the bed. His mind had refused to admit the possibility of even attempting sleep. And to put on pyjamas and slip between the crisp white sheets with the image of Housman, naked and bleeding among the dustbins, still clear in his mind had seemed a blasphemy. But his body had decided otherwise.

He drew back the curtains. Sunshine came in, weak but still dazzling. The bells stopped suddenly. It was Sunday morning and the first sitting at church had begun.

He stripped and went into the shower. The rush of water was sharp and refreshing, but inevitably it brought Housman back to mind. How was the man? He must surely have cracked some bones, though perhaps the stacked-up cardboard boxes might have broken his fall. He had certainly looked unconscious from the second-floor window. But it had been dark and he had not dared look for long. Not that it was much of a height, he reassured himself. You could jump out of a window like that, get up and walk away.

He dressed and went downstairs in search of a paper. The first three he looked at contained no mention of the incident. His spirits began to rise. It had been late, of course, but it would surely merit a mention if the injuries had been serious.

The fourth had a *stop press* column. It contained the simple statement. *A man fell to his death from a second-*

*floor room at the Kirriemuir Hotel last night. Police
have not yet ruled out foul play.*

He felt nothing, turned to the back page, looked at
the sports news. Then he turned the paper over again.
The words were still the same. He was seated in the
dining-room and the waiter now approached to take
his breakfast order, but he found it impossible to
contemplate being still.

"Later," he said, standing up and almost knocking
his chair over. He headed back to his room, eager to
examine what he felt. It was not guilt, or at least not
guilt pure and simple. At its simplest, the business had
been a dreadful accident, contributed to in no small
part by Housman's own aggression. But there was no
way of keeping things at their simplest. His presence
in the room had not been an accident. On one level it
was the result of a drunken impulse. Motorists whose
drunken impulses resulted in fatal accidents were tried
on a count only one stage less than murder. But at
another level, it had been an investigation, unofficial,
yes, and illegal too, but necessary—an investigation
into a suspected man's identity.

But on what flimsy grounds! The only piece of real
evidence, if it deserved that title, was the passport's
revelation that Housman had been in Peru. And that
knowledge was a result of the search, not one of its
causes.

Goldsmith found he was walking round and round
his room. The daemonic urge to activity which had led
him into such straits the previous night was again in
possession. He picked up the telephone and asked to
be connected with Templewood's hotel. It took only a
moment to get through but he was already tapping the
receiver rest impatiently. Mr. Templewood, he learned,
was out. No, they did not know when he might be
returning.

He left a message asking Templewood to ring him.
Probably the man had not been back to the hotel since
he left the reunion. He felt a twinge of the old teenage
envy of the man's sexual success, but also a near-

puritanical distaste at the thought of its attendant
indignities.

It would probably be wise to sit quietly now and
wait for Templewood to call. But he acknowledged
that this was beyond him. He had to get out and walk.
He thought longingly of the great empty expanses of
rolling countryside which lay outside his Yorkshire
home. What the hell was it that had made him agree
to let his name go forward on that short list? Success
would mean he would have to spend much of the year
down here in this ant-heap. Perhaps his initial decision
to stand as a local councillor had sprung from a sense
of the difference between what he had got and what so
many of those he now represented lacked. Or what he
lacked and what they had got. But to give up his sense
of space would be a gesture so futile as to be unre-
cognizable.

A police-car passed him, lights flashing, siren howl-
ing, and he stopped in his tracks. Housman was dead.
Housman had given everything up. His wife and child
would have been roused from their beds in the early
hours of this morning to be given the news. How
would they live with this new situation?

How would he live with it?.

He had made blunders before, bad decisions, and
survived. The resilience of the human spirit was tremendous, not just in the nice safe moral areas of
bearing grief or accepting sacrifice, but also in helping
man to survive self-knowledge. Kipling's "If" needed a
second section. A parody sprang half formed into his
mind.

> *If you can cheat the poor and still sleep soundly,*
> *Betray your friends and still laugh by their side,*
> *Destroy the joy of others, swearing roundly*
> *Nothing but good was meant to those who died*
> . . .

Yes, survival was always possible. Only in some
cases it came easier as the years passed. In others, not
so easy.

If Housman were Hebbel, that would make it easy. It was suddenly more important now than at any stage previously to establish the man's identity one way or another. And here in London on a Sunday morning, there was only one place he could make a start.

Half an hour later he was walking down Wath Grove. There was only one house on the left-hand side with scaffolding outside it and Housman had come out of the house before this. Its neighbour's face-lift accentuated its own shabbiness. The façade bore generations of London dirt and the paint was flaked and peeling from the front door. As he had surmised, the house was now divided into flats, and the yellowing slip of paper opposite the bell of the second-floor flat bore the name Sandra Phillips. He pressed it. A few seconds later the door opened and he went in.

The entrance hall was dark and smelled of fresh bacon and eggs and stale tobacco fumes. But the decoration looked new and the stairwell was in a good state of repair. The door to Sandra Phillips's flat had been newly painted, and the decorative amelioration clearly continued beyond from the glimpse he got when the door opened on a chain and a woman scrutinized him coldly from within.

"Yes?" she said.

Goldsmith looked at her speculatively. The simplest explanation of Housman's visit was that she was a prostitute. If that was the simple extent of their relationship, she could hardly help. But if their relationship were stronger than this, it was possible she might know something. The first thing was to test if she knew who Housman was.

"I'm a friend of Neil Housman's,' he said.

"Oh. You're a bit early." She made no move to open the door.

"I'm just in town this morning," he replied.

She continued to examine him with the same cold assessing gaze. He was being weighed in a balance and he had no idea what was in the other scale. Finally she closed the door without speaking and he thought he had failed the test. But she only wanted to unfasten the chain and when she opened the door again, her face was lit by a smile of real charm.

"Come in," she said. "The better the day, the better the deed, I suppose."

She was about his own age, he surmised, perhaps younger; a tall rangy woman with light brown hair which hung loose over her shoulders. She wore a housecoat with tiny blue and white checks, matching the décor of the kitchen which was visible through an open door to the left. Her face was free of make-up and she might have been part of an advert for butter or milk or cheese or anything healthy, rural, familial.

"I was just finishing breakfast," she said. "Like a coffee?"

"Thanks," he answered. She went into the kitchen and he examined the room he was in. As far as Sandra Phillips went, any shabbiness in this building stopped at her front door. The floor was highly polished woodblocking, strewn with rugs whose provenance Goldsmith was not equipped to guess at, but which looked exotically expensive. The furniture was a curious mixture. A large leather-upholstered sofa was flanked by a couple of ultra-modern armchairs. The lamp which hung over the elegant oval-shaped rosewood table might have come out of a space-ship. There was no sign of any morning paper anywhere.

"Like what you see?" asked the woman from the kitchen door. His examination must have been blatant.

"Yes," he said, taking the mug of coffee she offered him. "It's nice. Some good stuff. Then, I suppose, someone in Neil's position . . ."

He let his voice tail away. She smiled at him again, this time with no charm at all.

"I hope you haven't got the wrong impression from Neil. This stuff is mine, paid for by me. The lease of this place is in my name. And I pick and I choose and I get paid. I don't get loaned out for the weekend."

"No, of course not." He sipped his coffee. "This is good. Does it come as an extra?"

She looked at him thoughtfully, then decided to laugh.

"How long have you known Neil?" she asked, sitting down in one of the streamlined armchairs. Goldsmith sank into the leather sofa. Despite the estimated closeness of their ages, he felt they were correctly categorized by their choice of seating.

"A few years off and on," he said, grateful for this lead. "What about you?"

She didn't answer his question but said, "You didn't tell me your name."

"Maxwell," he said. "Jerry Maxwell. Has Neil ever mentioned me?"

"He doesn't talk about himself much," she said, adding with a smile, "not about himself now, anyway."

"More about his young days, you mean?" said Goldsmith casually, trying to control his excitement.

"That's what it's all about, isn't it?" she said enigmatically. "More coffee?"

"No, thanks. I get the impression that Neil spent a lot of time abroad when he was young."

"Do you? You'd better ask him yourself if you're interested. I charge high because I keep confidences. Well, if you've finished your coffee, we might as well start."

She stared at him evenly out of light blue eyes framed by unblemished white.

"If you want to start, that is."

Goldsmith felt uneasy. She was too astute for comfort. He momentarily considered confiding in her, but instantly dismissed the idea. Tarts with hearts of gold were as rare in his experience as virtuous women were to Solomon. He must avoid rousing her suspicions further. Eventually the news of Housman's death would reach her and she would think hard about her Sunday visitor. But unless there were strong emotional ties with the man (which on present evidence seemed unlikely) she would surely be reluctant to go to the police. Meanwhile he suspected she knew something of Housman's background and he wanted to find out what it was.

In any case he found that the thought of getting into

bed with this woman had begun to excite him. At least there was no risk of fiasco.

"Yes, I'd like to start," he said.

"Fine. Bedroom's through there. I'll be with you in a couple of minutes."

He listened carefully at the bedroom door for a while, suddenly suspicious that she might be ringing the police, or perhaps the Kirriemuir to get Housman to confirm he had sent Maxwell. But she busied herself in the kitchen for a few moments, then through the crack of the door he saw her go into what looked like the bathroom.

He turned now and examined the bedroom. The bed was large and luxurious, the other furniture simple and efficient. On the dressing-table a lidless jewel box glistened and shone like a child's treasure-chest. One of the wardrobe's sliding doors was half-open, revealing a line of clothes in close formation. The window looked down on Wath Grove itself, still not stirred from its Sunday morning somnolence. Puritanically he pulled the curtains tightly together and began to undress.

The bed proved to be as comfortable as it looked. The sheets were still warm from the woman's body and Goldsmith lay in a state of great physical excitement, Housman's fate and Housman's identity relegated to the depths of his mind for the time being. He heard the door open and closed his eyes. Footsteps approached and the bedclothes were pulled back from his body. He opened his eyes and looked up.

She was wearing a simple white blouse with puffed sleeves and a short grey skirt. Her hair had been plaited in two long pigtails which were pulled forward to hang over her breasts. In her hand she held a long bamboo cane with a split end.

She looked down at him in silence and he felt his desire failing.

"Interesting," she said, raised the cane and brought it down with all her strength across his knees.

"Jesus Christ!" he screamed, rolling out of the bed at the side opposite to her. She came round the bed

after him and caught him a stinging blow across the
shoulders before he could rise.

"There's been a mistake," he cried. She swung at
him again. This time he caught the cane in both hands
and wrenched it from her grasp. Slowly he rose and
they faced each other, only a couple of feet separating
them.

"Yes," she said. "You'd better get dressed, I think."

Once again the thought of confiding in her entered
his mind, this time more forcibly. Then the main door-
bell rang.

She went to the wardrobe, picked out a long silk
dressing-gown, slipped her arms into it and without a
glance at Goldsmith left the room. With self-defeating
haste he began to pull on his clothes. Whoever had
rung would have to climb the stairs and presumably
receive the same kind of scrutiny he had undergone.
Unless she had a minder of some kind and this was he.
Goldsmith was ignorant of such things and wanted to
be fully clothed when he found out.

There was a sharp rap at the flat door and he heard
Sandra open it on the chain.

"Yes," she said.

"Miss Phillips?"

"Yes."

"We're police officers. May we come in?"

"What's it about?" She did not sound impressed.

"We're investigating the death of a man called Housman, Miss Phillips. I believe you knew him. He had
your number in his diary. But we'd much rather talk
about it inside."

Goldsmith waited no longer. Sticking his tie in his
pocket and thrusting his arms into his jacket sleeves,
he moved at speed to the window and opened it. He
was two stories up, about the height which had killed
Housman. Parked outside the house was a blue 1300.
It was empty as far as he could make out. Its occupants must all have gone into the building.

The street itself was still quiet. A car went slowly
by, two children were playing about fifty yards away, a

dog waited patiently on a doorstep for someone to let
it in.

*Down* was not very attractive, *up* was clearly impossible. He stepped out on to the sill and launched
himself sideways.

There was no real danger. The decorators' scaffolding on the next building was only a matter of a yard or
so away. But he knew that if he had waited even a
second, he might have remained crouching on the sill
till the policemen pulled him back in.

He swung down from one level of scaffolding to the
next with an ease which reminded him of Tarzan's
exploits in the films of his childhood. Overconfidence
led him to hit the pavement with more force than he
intended. Winded and shaken, he pushed himself up
from his knees, which still ached from the woman's
assault, and set off at a discreet trot towards the busier
road on to which Wath Grove abutted.

The children did not even look up from their game.
Only the dog watched him go.

# CHAPTER VI

THERE WAS no message from Templewood, and when another call to his hotel produced the same result as before, Goldsmith packed, paid his bill and left.

He usually found that train journeys provided lots of space for thought and none for action, the ideal circumstances for studying problems from crossword puzzles to metaphysics. But today the carriage was full, his companions were loquacious and the movement of the train was interrupted by frequent halts. It was Sunday, explained a philosophical soldier. The day for repairs.

Goldsmith examined his feelings but found it a futile exercise. It was not what he felt now, his nerve edges still dulled by shock and this fitful journey north giving the illusion of separation from its source, but what he would feel later that mattered; when remembrance of Housman's body passing silently through the curtains brought him out of sleep to sit upright in bed at dead of night.

Suppose it had definitely been Hebbel. How much difference would that make? In theory, if all he and Templewood had said down the years was to be taken seriously, his only regret should then be that the killing had been accidental.

So, Housman or Hebbel, in either case I'm sorry it was an accidental death, he thought. The macabre paradox made him smile a little. It was well not to become too maudlin in his guilt. Not that there was much chance of that, he thought. A few hours after killing the man, I was itching to screw his tart.

But it did not matter whether guilt was going to climb into bed with him every night or merely tip its cap distantly from time to time. It was still important to know whether the dead man could really have been Nikolaus Hebbel.

The simplest course would be to give an anonymous tip to the authorities. Let the experts investigate. Maxwell's friends would dig through their records, perhaps produce fingerprints. And if there were a positive identification news would eventually reach him through the Colonel.

But such a course would be inviting trouble. Some bright policeman had only to spot that two of the potential main prosecution witnesses against Hebbel belonged to a regiment celebrating its annual reunion on the night of the death, and that would be that. He must have left his fingerprints all over Housman's room. The woman, Sandra Phillips, could identify him. And he had been stupid enough to give her Maxwell's name instead of saying he was Smith or Robinson.

So the situation remained as before. If he wished to know the truth, he would have to find it out for himself.

The tedious journey finally ended and he strode with relief from Leeds Station to the car-park where he had left his Land-Rover. The dusty, mud-caked vehicle suited him better than the glossy saloons among which he worked. As he approached it he noticed a piece of paper stuck behind one of the wipers and wondered if he had committed some subtle parking offence. He pulled it out and unfolded it.

*Spotted this junk heap while out shopping,* he read. *Why not try washing it? If you're back at a decent hour, call as you pass. Liz.*

He screwed the paper up and stuck it in his pocket. Elizabeth Sewell was another of his problems.

As an energetic, articulate and forthright woman, she made an excellent ward secretary and general organizer. But she was more than that and that was where the problems began.

For a start, she was his tenant. The old terraced

house in which Goldsmith had been born and which
his father had just finished paying for the year before
he died, had come to feel unbearably constricting. Ten
years earlier he had decided to move out. His career
in local politics was just starting and his friends were
dismayed when he told them he was moving right out
of the main conurbation. They had persuaded him not
to sell his old house, but to let it, so that his ownership
would continue to qualify him for membership of the
council. Liz had jumped at the chance of moving in,
and she shared the house with her mother, a smart
fifty-seven-year-old whose interest in seeing her daughter married to Goldsmith was matched only by Liz's
enthusiasm for the idea.

His route home took him past the house. He
was uncertain whether or not to stop, but the sight of
a blue-and-white Cortina parked in the road outside
made up his mind. It belonged to Jeff Malleson, the
local Party Secretary. If Jeff were out and about that
night, he would almost certainly end up at Goldsmith's
cottage and not care much about the time either.

Mrs. Sewell let him in, greeting him with a warm
hug. He disengaged himself with a smile which con-
cealed the uneasiness he sometimes felt at being alone
with her. The first time he had spent the night with Liz
under her own roof, he had been worried about Mrs.
Sewell's reaction. Liz had just laughed and put the
question direct to her mother, who had said that if he
was worried about climbing into Liz's bed, he was very
welcome to try hers first. He had never been certain
how much of a joke this was.

In the living-room, Liz was sprawled in characteristic fashion across a jumble of cushions on the floor.
Just as characteristically, Malleson was sitting at a card
table whose green baize was almost obliterated by
half-a-dozen neat piles of printed paper.

"The Hero returns," said Liz, smiling up at him
welcomingly. "How was the war? Did we win again?"

He ran his fingers through her dark brown hair
whose defiant untidiness sometimes amused, sometimes irritated him.

"Hello, Bill," said Malleson. "Just in time. I was going to call on you later to talk over next Thursday's meeting."

"Can it wait?" asked Goldsmith, sinking wearily into a chair. "I'm a bit knackered."

"It's these war games," mocked Liz, getting up. "I'll get Mam to do some coffee. Have you eaten?"

Goldsmith nodded. It was a lie, but he didn't feel hungry. He closed his eyes as Liz shouted instructions to her mother.

"Take no notice of Liz," said Malleson. "She's marched to Aldermaston too many times. Edmunds was asking where you were last night. He looked very approving when I told him."

Edmunds was the chairman of the candidate Selection Board, a loud, opinionated man whom Goldsmith found it hard to like.

"Did he?" he said. "That's nice."

"Now you can do yourself a bit of good at Thursday's meeting. All the committee'll be there of course, and you can dazzle them with your grasp of national issues and get old Barraclough on your side too."

Barraclough was the current Member of Parliament whose decision not to stand again had created the need for a new candidate. Malleson, a strong supporter of Goldsmith, was very proud that he had juggled things to get the two men on the same platform. Goldsmith himself doubted the wisdom of the move. Edmunds was not a man who liked to feel manœuvred.

"Are you sure it's a good idea, Jeff?" he asked again, adding on an impulse, "Are you sure the whole thing's a good idea? It'd take precious little to make me withdraw, I tell you."

"No!" protested Liz, who had returned unnoticed. "You mustn't! You withdraw and chances are that little LSE shit would worm his way in, him and his creepy wife both!"

"At least they can't hold a creepy wife against me," said Goldsmith. It wasn't a diplomatic thing to say, but he was too tired for diplomacy. The tensions and the travel of the past few days seemed to have sapped his last reserves of energy.

"I must be off on my travels," said Malleson rather too abruptly. "Ring you in the morning, Bill."

He gathered his papers together, placed them tidily in his briefcase and left, en route passing Mrs. Sewell plus coffee tray.

"Good night," he called. They heard the front door open and shut.

"Chased him off, have you?" asked Mrs. Sewell. "It's a wonder he didn't want to stay and watch. I've got my doubts about that one."

"Mam!" said Liz.

"I know what I know," said the other woman with a broad wink at Goldsmith. "I'm going to watch a bit of tele now. Behave yourselves!"

"She gets worse," said Liz after her mother had left.

"Yes," said Goldsmith.

"Did something happen in London?" asked Liz, observing him closely. He kept his eyes tight closed and forced himself not to react.

"Nothing unusual. Why do you ask?"

"You seem a bit, I don't know, unsettled. And you did go off unexpectedly early."

Who needs a police investigation if things stand out as clear as this? thought Goldsmith.

"No, I'm fine," he said, opening his eyes and smiling with an effort. "I've had a lousy migraine, that's all. Probably enjoyed myself too much last night."

She came and sat on the floor between his legs, full of solicitude.

"Can I get you anything?"

"No, thanks. A good night's sleep will see me right."

"You're probably overdoing things. You ought to have a word with your doctor."

"Doctors! The best they can do is put a name to what you're dying of."

"So? it's nice to know what kills us," she said lightly. "Anyway, stop being morbid! One bad headache doesn't mean you're marked for Paradise!"

"Don't intimations of mortality ever bother you?" he asked, trying to joke.

"I suppose. But not much. When it comes, it comes."

"It's not just when, it's *what*," he answered, almost talking to himself. "When men go to their death, what happens? Should we envy them or pity them? Are they losing or gaining?"

"It must depend on the man, surely?" she answered, turning and kneeling so that she could look into his face. "Bill, I don't think you should go home tonight. I don't fancy being by myself either. Will you stay?"

"I doubt if I'd be much good for you," he answered.

"Curiously, that wasn't what I had in mind. Just stay."

He had not planned to. Coming up on the train, solitude had seemed the only desirable, the only *possible* state. But now the thought of the uncurtained windows of the cottage staring blankly out into the darkness of the wooded garden, looking for his return, filled him with fear.

"All right," he said. "I'll stay."

He rose early the following morning, wanting to go home for a change of clothing before making his way to work. Liz, who had trouble with mornings, registered his going by grunting porcinely and rolling over. He admired the finely moulded planes of dorsal muscle and bone for a moment before quietly leaving the room.

Mrs. Sewell was sitting downstairs with a cup of tea and a cigarette.

"OK?" she said, enigmatically.

"Fine, thanks."

"Liz OK?"

"Yes. Shouldn't she be?"

"She *should* be," said the woman, dropping her stub into the tea-cup. "She *would* be if you married her."

"That's for us to decide," said Goldsmith, pretending an anger he didn't feel. She ignored him.

"Failing that, you could get out of the way and let

someone else have a chance at her. But marriage would be best," she acknowledged thoughtfully. "An MP needs a wife. Like a cup of tea?"

Goldsmith left without answering. His pretended anger moderated into an annoyance real enough to put the events of the weekend to the back of his mind until he arrived at his cottage simultaneously with the newspaper boy.

Housman's death was not brutal enough or dramatic enough to merit a headline, but an almost naked man falling out of a West End hotel window had sufficient curiosity value to fill an interesting paragraph on the front page.

He made himself a coffee and took it with him into the shower. As he was drying himself, the telephone rang. It was Templewood.

"Billy, have you seen the papers?" He sounded agitated.

"Yes."

"For Christ's sake, what happened?"

"What do you mean?" asked Goldsmith cautiously.

"I don't know what I mean. Look, after what we were talking about, I mean, could this be coincidence? That's what I wondered straightaway. I got your message yesterday, but when I rang, you'd checked out. Look, Billy, I'll come straight out, has this got anything to do with you? With what we were talking about?"

Despite his agitation, he's being very circumspect, thought Goldsmith. Not much here for eavesdroppers. He felt a perverse impulse not to co-operate.

"You mean, did I kill Housman?"

"Jesus wept! Listen, Billy, I can't talk now. We've got to meet. I can't get up to you before tomorrow lunch-time. Is there somewhere quiet we can meet?"

"If you like. There's a pub. The White Rose, Serlby Street. I can be there at one."

"That's fine. One o'clock. The White Rose. Are you all right, Billy?"

"Yes, fine. Why shouldn't I be?"

"That's good. See you tomorrow."

The phone went dead. Goldsmith replaced the receiver gently. Templewood's agitation had had a curious soothing effect on him, as though a responsibility had been shifted, temporarily at least.

He got dressed and went out into the back garden. It wasn't very big, a patch of neglected lawn with three or four apple trees rising from the rough cut grass. But the countryside ran away behind it to a long ridge which hinted at the imminent swell of the Dales. The view was uninterrupted yet, though the relentless city was in close pursuit elsewhere in the village. Soon it would be village no longer but just another expensive suburb. Goldsmith had bought his cottage ten years earlier at what had seemed then an absurd price for such a tumbledown building. But it was what he wanted and if he sold now, it would fetch six or seven times what he had paid. Only if the tentacles of brick and plate glass started coiling round behind him would he sell. He needed that space there.

He looked at his watch and whistled at the time. As he hurried to the Land-Rover he thought how nice it would be to have a single exclusive role in life, instead of this jumble of walk-on parts, dominated by the least important. There was much dramatic research to be done in the areas of William Goldsmith, uncertain politician; of Billy Goldsmith, hesitant lover; of ex-Private Goldsmith, W., DCM, killer. But it was Mr. Goldsmith, Chief Mechanic of Harewood Hire-Cars Ltd., who set them all breaking the speed limit through the morning traffic in order not to be late for work.

# CHAPTER VII

"ARE YOU SURE this isn't the gents?" said Templewood, looking round with distaste.

"You wanted somewhere we could talk," said Goldsmith equably.

The White Rose had few attractions as a lunch-time pub. It sold no food, it was big and draughty, everything about it was cold except the beer, and the use of mottled green and white tiles on the internal walls gave the bar the aspect of an unkempt aquarium.

The positive side of all these features was that you could get a table isolated from all possibility of eavesdropping.

Goldsmith pushed a pint towards the newly arrived Templewood and followed it with the offer of a paper bag containing two Cornish pasties.

"I brought an extra one in case you were hungry," he said.

"Thanks."

Templewood looked furtively round the room then leaned across the table and spoke in a low voice.

"What happened, Billy?"

"Are you sure you want to know?" asked Goldsmith.

"Don't be stupid! I've got to know."

"All right."

Briefly Goldsmith described the events of Saturday night. When he had finished they sat in silence for a while, drinking their acetic beer.

"Now you know, Tempy," said Goldsmith. "What do you suggest?"

"It's a mess. What can I say?"

"You can advise me. What do I do now? I could go to the police, I suppose."

Templewood looked alarmed.

"Why, for God's sake? That won't help."

"It's all right, Tempy. I wouldn't mention you," said Goldsmith with a wry grin.

"That's not the point. Look, it would finish you. Probably get you put away for five or six years at least. Put that right out of your mind, squire!"

"What do you suggest then? Do nothing?"

"Listen, Billy," said Templewood earnestly. "What else can you do? For the time being at least. Look at it this way, at worst it was an unfortunate accident, nothing more. And if by any chance, the fellow *was* Hebbel, then this was what we planned all along, wasn't it?"

"Maybe so. But we don't know, do we? You weren't in that room, were you? You were on the nest somewhere, nice and safe. But you started it, remember that!"

Goldsmith found he was speaking angrily, but he knew the anger was mostly directed at himself. He lowered his voice once more.

"We both need to know, Tempy. You must see that."

"OK. I concede that. But it's not worth getting yourself locked up for."

Briefly he outlined the same objections that Goldsmith had already worked out to any kind of anonymous tip-off. And he added a further one.

"Remember this too, Billy. If he did turn out to be Hebbel, that's a very good motive for murder, isn't it? Once a jury knew for certain, they'd begin to wonder if you weren't absolutely certain as well. You might get a lot of sympathy, but you'd still get sent down for a bigger slice of your life than you can afford to give at your age."

"So how do we find out?" asked Goldsmith.

"God knows. But just sit tight for the time being, Billy boy. I'll see if I can find out anything more about Housman through my business contacts. You never know. But you just keep your head down, concentrate on becoming Prime Minister. Anything crops up, ring me, OK?"

He handed over a business card. In the twenty years they had been more or less in touch, Goldsmith had never had a private address at which to contact Templewood. He sometimes wondered if perhaps the great lover had a nagging wife and clutch of squalling kids tucked away in some suburban villa.

Now Templewood rose to go.

"You didn't eat your Cornish pasty," observed Goldsmith.

"How do they ship them here? Round the Cape? I'll be in touch."

The brief encounter left Goldsmith with a sense of disappointment which lasted all afternoon. Despite the fact that over the years his ambivalent feelings for Templewood had set into an uncertain distaste, he still looked upon him as a man of proven ingenuity, a manipulator, a fixer. Some part of his being must have hoped that Templewood would come up with quick answers, though what possible answers were worth hoping for was difficult to imagine. Instead all he had encountered was an obviously worried man whose promises that he would put his mind to the problem were as reassuring as an alcoholic's vows of reform.

The rest of the week passed surprisingly swiftly. The kind of life he had built for himself left little time for brooding, though the darkness that rushed into his bedroom when he switched off the light seemed to grow thicker and more final each night, and the grey reassurance of the thin-curtained window took longer to eat its way through. The small wave of journalistic interest caused by Housman's death had faded almost instantly, and it was only by conscientiously reading every newspaper every day that he spotted that an inquest had been opened and adjourned. Presumably all the post-mortem examinations had been completed by now and the body would have been released for burial. The macabre thought crept into his mind that he might attend the funeral as an easy opportunity of checking on Housman's relations. It just needed one of his parents to be alive to put paid to any faint hope that he might actually have been Hebbel. But he pulled himself up short, horrified to find he was seriously contemplating such an intrusion. Or perhaps such a risk. Nevertheless the thought remained with him that the truth of the matter could only be uncovered in Sheffield.

The meeting on Thursday night went well. Perhaps just because his mind was far from being strictly focused on the business in hand, he spoke fluently and made a good impression on Edmunds and Barraclough.

Malleson and Liz were delighted and full of congratulations once they had parted company with the official party and were drinking pints of over-cooled beer in Liz's local.

"You might look a bit more pleased yourself," suggested Malleson.

"What? Sorry, but it wasn't exactly the United Nations, was it? A few dozen in the audience, and I knew most of them by name."

"Not the point. If there'd only been two, it would have been enough, as long as they were the right two. Another pint?"

Malleson went up to the bar and Liz leaned across and took Goldsmith's hands in hers.

"You've got it made," she said, smiling warmly. "When's the selection board?"

"Week after next."

"Great. Unless Edmunds catches you in bed with his wife, you can't miss."

"There are other candidates," protested Goldsmith.

"Mostly make-weights. Poor old Sanderson's so inarticulate, no one can understand him, and that little shit from LSE's so articulate everyone hates him. Which leaves you and Wardle."

"Who is dearly beloved in Transport House."

"Exactly! A lot of good that'll do him up here. You're a local lad. You know how obstinate *you* get when you think someone's trying to tell you what to do."

"Do I?" said Goldsmith reflectively. "The little shit's local too, isn't he?"

"In the sense that he was *born* here."

"What other sense is there?"

"Well, if his mother had dropped him in an aeroplane, that wouldn't make him a bloody albatross, would it?"

Goldsmith grinned, enjoying Liz's coarseness. But his mind was turning over memories of Housman's passport. Born in Sunderland. A distinctive accent, completely absent from Housman's husky voice. Not that that mattered. Voices changed, some more quickly than others. A man is little better than a dull-coloured parrot.

What did matter was that the North-East was a fiercely tribal area. Local memories would be long and specific. It shouldn't be difficult picking up traces of Neil Housman there.

"Councillor Goldsmith?"

He looked up, annoyed. His experience had taught him that this form of address in a public place frequently presaged unpleasantness. The speaker was a large red-faced man in a hairy suit. He looked vaguely familiar.

"Cyril Fell," he introduced himself. Goldsmith had him now. The senior partner of Fell and Fell, a small building concern who had on occasions done work for the council. The man was not drunk, but drink had polished his ruddy cheeks and brow till his face shone like a traffic light at stop.

"I would like to know," he said deliberately, "why Benson's got the Greengate Infant School job."

"Because they put in the lowest tender, I imagine," said Goldsmith equably.

"And why did they get the Thorpe House job?" continued Fell, swaying forward till he almost touched Goldsmith.

"Same reason. Look, Mr. Fell, I can't discuss council business here. Come and see me some other time, eh?''

"Lowest tender! I know that. But answer me this, Councillor Goldsmith. How did Benson know what the lowest tender needed to be? That'd be useful to know, wouldn't it? I'd like to know things like that!''

"Excuse me," said Malleson, returning from the bar with the drinks. "Hello, Mr. Fell. How's life? I thought I saw Mrs. Fell in the corner. Are you going to join us? I'll fetch her across, shall I?''

"No, thanks. We're on our way home," said Fell hastily. "You take heed of what I've said, Councillor. You're an honest man, I reckon, but take a good look at some of your friends in the Mayor's parlour.''

He turned and left.

"Thanks, Jeff," said Goldsmith.

"My pleasure. I knew if I suggested fetching his wife over, he'd be off in a flash! Moaning about missing out on council contracts, was he?''

"He was suggesting that someone's pushing things towards Benson's.''

"God! If these builders had their way, anyone who didn't accept their tenders would be shoved in the Tower of London instantly! Forget it, Bill. On second thoughts, mention it to Alf or someone, just to put yourself in the clear in case Fell goes too far one of these days. Well, sup up. Here's to the General Election. Next spring would be my bet. And this time we'll have the bastards out!''

Despite the fact that none of Fell's accusations had been directed at himself, Goldsmith found that the incident soured the evening for him. He refused Liz's invitation to have coffee at her house and pointed the Land-Rover home with a faintly guilty sense of relief. His companions' euphoria had been rather wearing. He was far from clear about his own reason for being involved in public life, but he would have denied either of the clichés of political motivation—the lust for power or the longing for service. In the presence of the fully committed he always felt out of place, bogus almost. He had the time, it filled a gap in his life, and he was good at it—that was as far as he was willing to go in analysing his own commitment, even to himself. He smiled at the irony of it all. The country must be full of MP's manqués, desperate for adoption, and here was William Goldsmith finding it rather distasteful to be on a short list.

But then, not many of these other would-be politicians had five days earlier hurled a man to his death from a hotel window.

That night he took three aspirins washed down with a tumblerful of scotch and went to bed, resolving to take Templewood's advice to put Housman out of his mind and concentrate on sorting out his public career.

Friday morning was bright and crisp and suddenly it seemed possible. He felt better than he had done all week as he entered the general office of Harewood Hire-Cars. He had been with the firm for thirteen years now, joining it when it was relatively small and doubling up as a driver and mechanic. Now he had the title Chief Mechanic, but in fact, had he wished, he could have spent all his time behind a desk acting as under-manager. But he clung fiercely to his right to cover himself with sump-oil or put on a peaked cap and chauffeur the firm's customers if he so desired.

Today he organized a ferocious attack on the paperwork that awaited him, planning to spend a couple of hours in overalls before the day was out. As therapy, it worked; London was a million miles away till suddenly halfway through the morning, Janet, the general secretary sitting at the far side of the room, put down the phone, stood up, walked over to him, waited till her presence brought his head up from the papers he was immersed in and said, "Cancel Housman."

For a second he thought he was in a dream.

"What?"

"Housman. This afternoon. A pick-up from the airport. J. T. Hardy's booking. Cancelled."

"What?" he repeated.

"You've got the book," the girl said patiently. "They've just rung up to cancel. A bit late really.

Shall we charge the cancellation fee? Are you all right, Mr. Goldsmith?''

He reached for the booking log and opened it. There it was. *Mr. N. Housman, 3:30, Leeds Airport. Bill J. T. Hardy's (Sheffield) Ltd.*

He ignored the girl, got up, and went to the washroom and looked at himself in the mirror. The coincidence had shaken him visibly. *Cancel Housman.*

*I have, I have,* he thought, bathing his face in cold water. He felt helpless, a slave of chance.

The darkness that night was thicker and longer lasting than ever before. In the end, after a few desperate mouth-drying moments spent groping for the switch, he put the light on again.

It was, he decided, no use waiting for Templewood to delve into Housman's background. He had to find out for himself. His diary for the coming weekend was full of appointments but they would have to wait. He was going to Sheffield.

He got up, switched on the landing light and returned to bed. The line of brightness beneath the door cut through the blackness of the bedroom when he turned off his bedside lamp once more and he fell to sleep, remembering his childhood.

# CHAPTER VIII

THE HOUSE WAS a substantial Edwardian villa in dark red brick caught in a net of Virginia creeper. The chimney-stacks were so tall and narrow and the steeply-angled roof was pinched so frequently into dormer windows that despite the basic solidity of the building, it sat in its lawns like a fragile ship waiting for fair winds and a favourable tide.

The grass had that elegantly razed look which says "care" or "wealth," depending on the size of the garden. Greenmansion was far from a stately home, but there was more work here than an amateur enthusiast could manage, even with a motor-mower.

Goldsmith let his gaze move slowly round the garden, relaxing his eyes in the variegated greens, punctuated from time to time with bursts of colour from late-flowering shrubs and plants. He was no horticulturalist and could identify very little other than a pair of rowan trees, beaded red among their serrated leaves.

There was no sign of movement in the garden or house. No smoke rose from the chimneys, no one moved behind the blank glass of the windows. It was from just such a house as this that a sad little rich boy had gazed in an illustration to some long-forgotten story-book of Goldsmith's childhood. The title still escaped him but the picture came back now with complete clarity. Housman had a daughter, he recalled. Perhaps somewhere inside she was sitting now, motionless and in silence.

So rapt was he in his meditations that he did not notice the police car coming towards him till it was

almost opposite. Its left indicator was flashing as though
it were going to turn into the drive of Greenmansion,
but instead it came to a halt before the gates. A tall
angular man unfolded himself from the passenger seat
and stood staring across the road at Goldsmith. He
felt greatly tempted to start the engine and drive away
but his mind told him this would be a foolish thing to
do. It would look suspicious, they would check his car
number and set in train a routine investigation which
might lead . . . where might it lead? His mind raced
now; they might have a description of him from the
woman in Wath Grove; fingerprints even; he must
have touched something in the flat. If the man in
charge of the main investigation should notice a resemblance between Sandra Phillips's description and
the watcher in the Land-Rover, it would take very
little probing to reach the truth of what had happened.
Or at least the truth as it would seem to the police.

He opened the door, stepped down from the Land-
Rover and strode smartly across the road. The tall
man watched his approach imperturbably.

"Excuse me," said Goldsmith. "But this is Neil
Housman's house? I wasn't certain, then I saw you . . ."

He tailed off invitingly, but the tall man offered no
help. Goldsmith felt himself being pressured into a
rambling, revealing course of explanation and apology. With an effort of will he resisted it and after a
moment's silence, raising his voice to a level of polite
acerbity, asked, "Well, is it?"

"That's right, sir. May I ask who you are?" The tall
man's voice was like his face, expressionless.

"My name's Goldsmith. And you?"

"Vickers, sir. Detective-Inspector. You were a friend
of Mr. Housman?"

"Yes. Not very close, it's some time since I saw
him. Then I read about it in the papers and, well,
naturally I was shocked. I saw the address and as I was
coming out this way, I thought I might call to express
condolences. To tell you the truth, I was really trying
to summon up courage. It's not easy, and you never
know, intruding on grief, that kind of thing."

I'm doing it, he thought in surprise. Rambling, ex-plaining, over-elaborating. So much for self-control.

"You know Mrs. Housman, sir?"

"No. That's it, you see. I never met her. Look, are you going to be very long?"

"Just a couple of minutes, sir. We might as well walk up to the house together."

Their feet crunched in the gravel drive. Vickers took long, loping strides and Goldsmith found himself adjusting his own stride pattern in an attempt to syn-chronize their steps.

"Was it an accident, Inspector?" he asked suddenly. "What really happened?"

"If we knew that," began Vickers, but the front door opened at that moment and he paused. Out came a girl, just the sort of young girl Goldsmith would have expected to issue from such a house in his story-book. About twelve years old, she had long, thin-spun, wheat-blonde hair which fell in a tangle of light over her back and shoulders. She wore a simple black dress with lace at the cuffs and throat. Her features were regular and intelligent, and she stood by the door, watching their approach with quiet grey eyes.

Goldsmith's stride faltered for a moment. He recog-nized her from the photograph in her father's bed-room and he recalled the string of beads Housman had bought.

"Hello, Dora. Is your mother in?" asked Vickers. His voice became genial. It was like hearing another man speaking.

She nodded and stood aside, pushing the door open. They entered the house.

"Mrs. Housman!" called Vickers.

Ahead of them at the far end of the spacious, pan-eled hall, a door opened and a woman appeared.

She too wore a simple black dress but unrelieved by any white lace. Her hair was also black, cut very short around her small, delicate head. Only her eyes had been passed down to her daughter, large and grey.

She nodded at Vickers and glanced incuriously at Goldsmith who would have been very glad to stay quietly in the background. But the Inspector looked at him expectantly and it was impossible not to speak.

"Mrs. Housman," he said, "I'm William Goldsmith; your husband may have mentioned me."

He did not pause long enough for a positive denial but pressed on apace, feeling like an amateur actor suddenly thrust under the scrutiny of top theatre critics.

"I was most distressed when I read about the . . . the accident. As I was in the neighbourhood, I thought I would call to say . . . I hope you don't mind."

"Of course not. It's most kind. Mr. Goldsmith, did you say? Please come in."

Her voice was high but pure in tone. She led them into a large drawing-room which looked out from the back of the house. The same variegated swathes of lawn ran away to a line of rose-bushes, still heavy with colour.

"I don't recollect my husband mentioning you, Mr. Goldsmith. But he spoke of so many people. Had you known him long?"

"Not long, I'm afraid," he answered lamely.

"Then it's all the kinder of you to call."

Goldsmith found it impossible not to glance towards Vickers to observe his reaction to the exchange. Mrs. Housman must have noticed the flicker of the eyes and perhaps misinterpreted it, as now she turned to the inspector and asked, "How can I help you, Mr. Vickers? Will it take much time?"

"Hardly a moment."

"Then perhaps you won't mind hanging on for a while, Mr. Goldsmith? Please sit down. I look forward to talking with you."

Vickers followed her out with a last assessing glance at Goldsmith who sank into an armchair, sighing with relief at being left alone. It did not last long. He realized he was assuming that Vickers was a local man, unconnected with the London end of the investigation. But why should this be so? Perhaps already in his mind he was ticking off points of resemblance between the Phillips woman's description and the man he had spotted so suspiciously watching the house from a parked car.

Goldsmith stood up. Action was better than this disturbing and unproductive speculation. Now he was in the house, he might as well do what checking he could on Housman's antecedents.

It seemed at first as if this room was going to offer very little help. There was an elegant mahogany bureau opposite the door but it proved to be locked. A wall cabinet was open, but contained only some glasses and a bottle of sherry. But as he moved away from it, he glimpsed something on top of it, pushed back almost out of sight. He reached up and took hold of a photograph in an old silver frame, heavy enough to be genuine. The picture was of a post-christening scene. Mrs. Housman was holding a baby, presumably Dora, with four adults grouped symmetrically around her, a man and a woman on either side. One couple were middle-aged, the other younger.

Relations. That was the simple proof. Relations who would gather at family festivals. A christening. Or a funeral. It just needed a couple of maiden aunts from Harrogate to have been present at their favourite nephew's funeral, and that was that. Investigation over.

"Are you a policeman?"

He started, nearly dropping the photograph, and turned. It was the girl, who had come so silently into the room that she had been able to close the door behind her undetected.

"Hello," he said. "No, I'm not a policeman. I used to know your daddy, your father. So I thought I'd call."

He had little experience of talking to children and found he had put on a kind of bright bluffness, like a conscientious Santa Claus in a big store magic grot.

"I'm Dora," she said. "What's your name?"

"William Goldsmith," he answered. She came forward and held out her hand. He transferred the photograph from one hand to the other and shook hands.

"That was at my christening," said Dora gravely.

"I thought it must be," said Goldsmith. There might

be a chance here, he realized. Another few seconds might convince him once and for all that an innocent man had died.

"Are these your grandparents?" he asked.

"Those are," said Dora, pointing at the elderly couple. "The others are my godparents. They should help me with my catechism, but they just send money."

"That can't be bad," said Goldsmith. "Are they your mother's parents."

"That's right."

"What about your father?"

"I think he was probably taking the picture," she said thoughtfully. "He doesn't like being photographed. Didn't like."

She repeated the words slowly as if sampling the change of tense. Her self-possession was a fragile thing, realized Goldsmith. But he felt unable to stop now.

"I meant, weren't your father's parents at your christening?" he said gently.

"I'm not sure."

"Neil's parents died in the war, Mr. Goldsmith."

It was Mrs. Housman. Silent entrances were obviously much practised in this house. She came forward from the open door and touched her daughter on the shoulder.

"Run along now, darling. I want to talk with Mr. Goldsmith."

The girl held out her hand once more.

"Goodbye," she said as Goldsmith took it. As she closed the door behind her, her mother said, "She's become incredibly formal in the past week. Everything correct and polite. It's a formal time, don't you think, Mr. Goldsmith? A time of strict traditional procedures. Dora seems to be seeking a kind of permanent shelter in them, but it won't work for ever."

"I'm sorry," said Goldsmith. This wasn't what he had foreseen, if indeed he had foreseen anything when he got into the Land-Rover that morning. The sooner he got out of this house the better. He wanted these two females to remain two-dimensional, just snapshots seen in a hotel bedroom. But already it was too late for that.

"How long had you known Neil?" asked the woman, sitting down and motioning Goldsmith to do the same.

"Not long. Oh, eighteen months, couple of years at the most," answered Goldsmith. He felt that it was desperately unfair. The lies he told now were the lies he would have to live with, for the next few minutes at least. Or substantiate if Vickers decided he was worth investigation. And he had no time to shape them, to weigh them, to look at their implications.

"Where did you meet him?" she asked now. "You're not a local man, are you, Mr. Goldsmith?"

It was more than just a question of geography, he realized. She meant that had he been a local man in any sense, her husband would surely have mentioned him at some point.

"No. Well, I am a Yorkshireman, yes, but it was in London we met."

There was nowhere else he could say. If they hadn't met locally, London was the only possible place. Where else would Housman have made regular trips?

"London? You didn't see him on his last trip, did you?"

Her voice was as calm and polite as if she were talking about a man who might at any moment walk through the door and pour himself a drink.

"I'm afraid not. I'm not centred there, you understand."

The questions were fast becoming impossible. Soon he would have to start creating a mass of circumstantial detail, any part of which might trip him up. He decided to take the initiative.

"I nearly didn't come in," he said. "When I saw the police car, I thought, well, you must have enough on your plate. It's bad enough losing someone without all the fuss of an investigation."

"I'm glad you called just the same," she answered. "The police have been no trouble, you understand; perfectly polite. But it's their job to probe, I suppose."

"Do they know yet what did happen?"

She looked directly at him. Her eyes seemed almost too big for the small-boned head.

"No. I doubt if they ever will. I believe it was just an accident. Neil worked too hard. Occasionally he had dizzy spells, perhaps more frequently than he told me."

"I'm sure you are right," said Goldsmith. "Are you by yourself?"

The question must have come out rather too bluntly. She looked at him in slight surprise.

"Yes. Why?"

"I'm sorry, I just thought you might have someone staying with you. Your parents, perhaps. Or some of Neil's relations."

"No. My mother came down earlier in the week, but she couldn't stay. My father's ill and needs looking after. They're all the relations I've got in the world except for a few distant cousins. And Neil had none at all. I never knew anyone so relation-free."

She smiled reminiscently, the first smile Goldsmith had seen on her face. For a moment the tightness round the mouth and eyes disappeared and she looked ten years younger. Goldsmith would have liked to encourage the mood, but it was not an opportunity to be missed.

"Surely he must have produced someone at your wedding?" he asked.

The smile died. She shook her head.

"No. No one. It was a quiet affair, but there was no one at all from Neil's side. I thought, it must be strange to have no relations."

She said nothing further, but lapsed into an introspective silence which did not invite interruption.

Goldsmith glanced ostentatiously at his watch. It was time to go, he felt. His luck had held so far and though he had learned nothing, negatives in this instance were on his side.

"I'm afraid I must be on my way," he said, standing up.

"Must you? I was hoping you might have some tea with us."

"Another time perhaps," Goldsmith heard himself saying.

"Yes. Please call again if you can," she answered, offering her hand in a gesture so like her daughter's that he felt momentarily moved by the thought of the grief that might lie inside.

But simultaneously the thought rose in his mind that this hand he held might have touched and caressed the supple body of Nikolaus Hebbel.

"I should like that," he said. "There's so much to talk about."

# CHAPTER IX

SUNDAY WAS WET and Goldsmith spent the morning in fitful attempts to do some paper-work. He had a standing invitation to lunch with Liz and her mother, but when Mrs. Sewell rang to check at eleven o'clock, he pleaded pressure of work and offered his apologies with a minimum of courtesy. At twelve he made his way to the local pub and ate a pork-pie. As the place began to fill up, he rose and headed for the door, reluctant to be drawn into conversation with any of the new arrivals. But outside he bumped into Cyril Fell, the builder, who detained him with a hand like a fire-shovel. His intentions were far from aggressive, however.

"Mr. Goldsmith," he said gruffly, "sorry I bothered you the other night. It wasn't the place, but you know how it is."

"Yes," said Goldsmith, turning up the collar of his sheepskin jacket against the rain.

"Mind you, I still think there's something fishy, that I do," added the man emphatically.

"Then you must inform the police," said Goldsmith.

"Police? What's them buggers got to do with it? It's a council matter."

"What you're suggesting is misuse of public monies and that's a criminal matter, Mr. Fell. Look, if you want to talk about this any more, come up to my cottage in half an hour."

He pushed aside the builder's restraining hand and made for home.

By two o'clock, Fell still had not arrived and Goldsmith was in no mood for waiting. The rain had slackened slightly and he was tired of the confines of his house. Putting on his still damp jacket, he went out of the back door and clambered through the hedge at the bottom of his garden. The land here sloped up to a lightly wooded ridge, then fell away into a stony valley through which ran a noisy stream not yet tamed from its moorland sources. There were outcrops of rock even on this side of the ridge and the land was only useful for grazing sheep. This meant there was no need for fences or hedges, much to Goldsmith's satisfaction. He did not count the mossy drystone wall over to his left which marked the line of the lane running up to the farm house on the other side of the valley. He wished his own cottage had been on that side too. When the stream was in spate, the ford where the lane crossed it was often impassable, and access to the farm was only possible via a long and unattractive detour.

The rain came on again as he reached the trees on top of the ridge. Three of them had been blasted by lightning four or five years earlier and every strong wind brought new billets of dead timber crashing down. But they were too far from the lane to be regarded as dangerous and were allowed to remain as a natural frieze, picturesque against the summer sky and Gothic against the winter moon.

Goldsmith sheltered against one of them and looked back towards his cottage and the road. A white Volkswagen Beetle made its way slowly along, its distinctive roof just visible above the hedge. It disappeared behind the cottage but did not emerge on the other side. Goldsmith watched for five minutes before he saw it reappear and return the way it had come. Someone had called on him. Goldsmith did not recognize the car, nor did he feel interested enough even to speculate.

Turning his back, he leaned against the carbonized trunk of the tree and stared down into the valley till the damp penetrated to his skin and the warmth of the cottage became attractive again.

The following morning he telephoned the firm and

told them he had caught a chill and would not be going in that day. In retribution, he began to sneeze as he drove north shortly afterwards, but he ignored the symptoms and by mid-morning the Land-Rover was edging its way through the cold and windy streets of Sunderland.

He had been uncertain how best to go about obtaining the details he would need to check on Neil Housman's background and had prepared a variety of (to him) implausible-sounding cover stories, but his request for a copy of the birth-certificate was received without comment at the Registrar's office.

He went into a café, ordered a cup of tea, and examined his new information with interest. At least Neil Housman existed. Or had existed.

Neil Housman. Born November 11th, 1918. Father, Andrew Housman, shop-keeper, of 99, Byron Lane, Sunderland. Mother, Enid Housman, housewife.

He finished his tea and went in search of a stationery shop where he bought a street map of the town. There was only one Byron Lane and after two or three false starts, he finally reached it, only to find himself looking at two rows of houses which clearly had been built since the end of the war.

A postman was walking along the pavement and Goldsmith leaned out of the Land-Rover window and called to him.

"It's the old Byron Lane you're wanting," said the man after listening to Goldsmith's question. "That was here all right, but it's been knocked down these ten years or more."

"Where did the people who lived there go?" asked Goldsmith.

"Now you're asking," replied the postman. "All over, I reckon,"

"Not to these homes then?"

"How could they?" said the man scornfully. "They didn't just build these places overnight, man. It'd be a year or more between getting the people out and these houses being ready to live in."

After a final assurance that there was no one in this

or any of the neighbouring streets called Housman, the postman strode away, leaving Goldsmith feeling absurdly dejected. He was discovering that once you commit yourself to a line of detective work, the actual deductive process can become more important than the reasons for embarking upon it.

Leaving the Land-Rover, he walked the length of the street wondering what his next move should be. On an impulse, he marched up the path of No. 99 and rang the bell. A small, faded woman came to the door. Her answers were as dusty as her appearance.

No, she knew nothing about previous inhabitants of the street. No, she knew no one in the street who might help. No, she knew nobody called Housman.

Eventually he gave up and returned to his vehicle. He was ready to abandon the chase and leave these ugly streets behind. Not even the not-too-distant tang of the sea could combat the depressive effect this place was having on him. But as he switched on he heard a voice calling and, looking around, he saw the faded woman waving to him from her garden gate. Slowly he drove alongside her and halted, not switching off the engine.

"Yes?" he said.

"I just remembered," she said. "My old dad used to say he was calling in at Housman's when he was going to that little shop in Arundel Street. It's not Housman's really but Billington's, something like that. Still, he always used to say Housman's."

"Did he? Is Arundel Street far? Could I speak to your father perhaps."

She laughed, like light shining through a threadbare curtain.

"You'll have to go a lot farther than Arundel Street. He passed on seven years ago. Take the first left, then keep on down to the traffic lights, then right. Billingham's, is it?"

"Thank you very much," said Goldsmith.

She was right first time. J. S. Billington said the sign above the door. The shop sold newspapers, sweets, basic groceries. It was set in a terrace of houses much older than the new Byron Lane and Goldsmith began to feel hopeful. The birth certificate had said that Housman senior was a shopkeeper.

He went in and the discordant jangle of the old-fashioned bell was like the splintering of time as he stepped out of the supermarket age.

A man in his fifties came out of the shadowy rear section of the shop. He had a thin inquiring face and wore a grey cap, set jauntily on one side of his head.

Goldsmith bought a bar of chocolate, hesitating over his choice. He had the feeling that the man recognized his hesitation for the play-acting it was, and certainly when Goldsmith finally said, "This place used to belong to the Housmans, didn't it?" his nod seemed as much an act of self-congratulation as of acquiescence.

"When did they leave?" Goldsmith asked next.

"Let me see. The year the war ended," answered the man, setting his head on one side so that the cap was almost perpendicular.

"Are they still living locally?"

"Well, they're local, I suppose you could say. Just round the corner. St. Columba's."

These people seemed to be easily amused by death, thought Goldsmith.

"There was a boy, wasn't there?" he said.

"I think there was. Yes, I think they mentioned him. He would still be in the Army, I suppose, when I bought the place. I never went myself. Had a bad back."

He sounded regretful rather than apologetic.

"Didn't he come for the funeral?"

The man laughed. Death again, thought Goldsmith.

"I don't know. Perhaps there was enough dead where he was. Anyway, I never saw him, then or after."

"Did the Housmans live above the shop?"

"Where else would they live?"

"I thought they once lived in Byron Lane."

The man whistled.

"You're going a long way back. They moved from there before the war."

"And where did they go from here?"

"I told you. St. Columba's. Oh, they had some idea of taking a place on the coast Seaham way. But they both went like that. A road accident. God knows where he got the petrol! He was just sixty, I reckon; she was a bit younger."

He shook his head as though at some avoidable human frailty.

Goldsmith picked up his chocolate and turned to go. This looked like another dead end. But his mind was beginning to be attuned to the special demands of detection now, and at the door he stopped and asked, "When you bought the place, you'd need a solicitor, I suppose. Do you remember who the Housmans' solicitor was?"

"Oh yes. I remember that. Same as mine, one man did both jobs, money for breathing that was."

"He wouldn't *still* be breathing, would he?"

The man did not miss the irony, but was neither offended nor amused by it.

"Simpson," he said. "Blackstone Road. He'll have the silver paper off your chocolate if you don't watch him."

Five minutes in Simpson's company made Goldsmith begin to accept the truth of Billington's assessment. Simpson was ancient, his skin leathery as a tortoise's neck, but the eyes were bright and missed nothing. There was a young partner who it appeared did all the work. Theoretically Simpson himself had retired, Goldsmith gathered, but the lure of other people's problems was strong.

"All I do is listen, Mr. Maxwell. That's all. No paper-work, can't stand paper-work, never could. Now I don't have to."

He laughed, his face folding into creases so deep that it seemed each spasm of amusement might break through the skin to the sharp bones beneath.

"Now, Mr. Maxwell," he said finally. "Now, Mr. Maxwell. You were saying?"

There was something mocking in his repetition of the name. Goldsmith had decided at the last moment it was foolish to reveal his identity unnecessarily and

Maxwell had once again been the first name to come
to mind. It was a habit he would have to break.

"I'm trying to trace an old friend. Neil Housman.
We lost touch shortly after the war. I've been round to
the shop his parents used to keep in Arundel Street,
but there's someone else there now, Mr. Billington.
He gave me your name."

"And how do you think I can help, Mr. Maxwell?"

"I thought, if there had been a will when the old
people died and Neil inherited, well, you might have
had an address, something to start a trail."

"A trail, eh? Sounds interesting. A trail. You'll
pardon my curiosity I'm sure, Mr. Maxwelton . . ."

"Maxwell."

". . . of course; but why do you want to find Mr.
Housman? A matter of money, is it?"

"Just friendship. We lost touch, I was up here, so I
thought . . ."

"I see." The bright eyes flickered cynically upwards
for a moment. "I see. You were imprisoned with him
perhaps?"

Goldsmith sat up in his chair so violently that it
scraped across the floor. He knew it was impossible,
but suddenly it felt as if the old man knew everything
about him.

"Imprisoned?" he repeated.

"Yes. If it's the right Housman I'm thinking of,
their son was in a POW camp. Well, we'll soon find
out."

He rang a small handbell on his desk and a young
clerk appeared at the door.

"In the cupboard in the cloakroom you may, if you
are both energetic and lucky, find a file marked Housman. Bring it, please."

The clerk left and Simpson arranged his creases into
a social smile.

"Now we must merely await the event, Mr. Macbeth."

"Maxwell."

"I'm sorry. Still it's all Scottish. There's no art to
find the name's construction in the face, eh? Where do
you hail from, Mr. Maxwell?"

"London. I work in London," said Goldsmith.

"London. Where precisely may I ask? I used to know London well. I was articled there, you know. Happy days. Interesting stuff I used to be in touch with. Criminal. I fancied myself as a criminal specialist, but like most of us I ended up with half a century of conveyancing. Where did you say you worked?"

The phone rang, saving Goldsmith from the intellectual pains of further lying. Simpson had a conversation about the possibility of making up a bridge four that evening, and as he finished the clerk returned with the file.

"Now we shall see," said Simpson, opening it. For a few moments he thumbed through the papers it contained, his face expressionless.

"Yes," he said finally. "This is the one. There was a will, I see. Everything to their only son, Neil. There was some delay as he was still away. The young man evidently spent some time in hospital after his liberation."

"Do you know what was wrong?" asked Goldsmith.

"Undernourishment, the usual POW thing, I suppose. No. Wait a minute. There's something here. He was wounded. In the neck."

"Was he? Look, Mr. Simpson, I know it's a long time, but do you recall anything about him, about his appearance I mean?"

It was a foolish question, no answer to it could be helpful, and Simpson was looking at him with open curiosity.

"No, I don't," he answered. "Which is not surprising as I never saw the young man. All the details were settled by letter as far as I can make out. It dragged on for some time."

"By letter? Then you'll have an address."

Some military hospital, he thought. Or at best an army camp.

"Indeed I do. Several. But the last is what you'll want of course."

He shuffled the papers. "Here we are, though what

use it will be, I do not know. It's nearly twenty years old after all."

"Could I have it, anyway?"

"Of course. Here we are. Neil Housman. 26, Culham Gardens."

"Sunderland?"

"Oh no. Not Sunderland, Mr. MacHeath. Leeds."

# CHAPTER X

IT WAS POSSIBLE, the heavy beat of the Land-Rover's engine seemed to insist all the way down the A1.

The war grinding to an end. Hebbel back in Germany checking carefully through POW records to find a face that fitted, a background that presented no difficulties. Perhaps Housman was on a short list already. Then news of his parents' death reached the camp and he went to the top of the list. A transfer is fixed. Easy enough for Hebbel. Housman leaves Camp A. Shortly afterwards Hebbel is delivered to Camp B with a nasty throat wound, and lies speechless in the camp hospital till liberation.

No, it's absurd; he told himself in a sudden change of mood. He would need accomplices and could such a wound as had caused that dreadful scar on Housman's neck be self-inflicted?

He turned off the A1 and drove towards Ripon. It was not the quickest way home, but he was in no hurry and felt in the mood for narrow winding "B" roads and unclassified tracks which were more like creases in the ancient skin of the moorlands than intrusions upon it. The image made him think of Simpson, the old solicitor. Was he as astute and perceptive as he seemed? Or was this merely a sophisticated form of that typical Northern "knowingness" which stems from inbred suspicion of the motives of strangers? He wasn't free of it himself. Readiness to suspect the worst had got him into this business to start with.

He treated himself to afternoon tea at a small hotel near Pateley Bridge where the waiter was either a dwarf or should have been at school. Afterwards he walked a couple of miles over the fields till a flurry of rain made him turn back to the road.

It was dusk when he arrived home. He felt weary, and as he unlocked the door he was looking forward to sinking into the huge soft leather armchair which was one of his few furnishing extravagances. But his mood changed as soon as he stepped into the hall.

Someone had been here. There was no noise, movement, smell, nothing to advertise the intrusion so immediately. But he felt it.

And there *was* something tangible, he realized as he moved cautiously along the hallway. A current of air that shouldn't have been.

The kitchen door was ajar. He pushed it fully open and saw at once the source of the draught. Someone had smashed in a pane of glass from the window. With that out of the way, it would be an easy task to reach in and open the window. There were traces of mud on the window-sill where the intruder had scraped his foot. Goldsmith felt at the same time very angry and very frightened. Angry at the fact of intrusion, frightened at its possible motives.

Behind him someone coughed.

He turned so quickly he caught his knee on the kitchen table and staggered against it for support as his leg buckled.

Standing in the dark rectangle of the doorway wearing a short white raincoat which his height made look like a jacket was a man.

There was a drawer in the table. In it Goldsmith kept his cutlery, including a fearsome broad-bladed carving knife. It was this that came into his mind now as he slowly reached for the drawer.

"Hello, Mr. Goldsmith. Sorry if I startled you, but the front door was open."

The man stepped forward into the kitchen, Goldsmith had the drawer open but his fingers halted short of the knife. The last glimmers of light falling through the broken window showed him the man's face. It was Inspector Vickers.

"Good evening, Inspector," said Goldsmith, casually drawing the curtains of the broken window. "What can I do for you?"

"Nothing. It's daft really," Vickers said with a convincing laugh. "I suppose I'm just making sure you are *you*."

"I'm sorry?"

"Well, I'll come clean with you, shall I? It's my rest day and there is nothing I like more than a stroll in the Dales. On my way home, I suddenly thought of you. You know, when a man dies and it gets in the paper, especially a well-to-do man like Mr. Housman, you often get some very strange characters turning up and bothering the widow."

"And you thought . . ."

"Not really. But while I was up here, it seemed worth while just checking you were who you said."

"And this proves I'm not a strange character?" asked Goldsmith, wondering what degree of indignation was proper for such a scene. He frequently found himself carefully measuring certain public emotions—sorrow, amusement, enthusiasm—and felt that in this at least he was a true politician.

"Probably," replied Vickers. "Such people don't usually identify themselves so readily. Unless they're very strange characters indeed."

"Would you like a cup of tea, Inspector?" asked Goldsmith. "Or perhaps a drink as you're not on duty?"

"That would be kind, though I mustn't keep you long. It must be pretty time-consuming being in politics as well as doing a full-time job."

"It sometimes is," said Goldsmith, producing a bottle of scotch from the cupboard under the sink. He made no effort to take his unwanted guest into the living-room where for all he knew unmistakable evidence of the break-in might abound, but placed his glass on the kitchen table and invited him to pull out a stool.

"Anything more on poor Housman's death?" asked Goldsmith.

"Nothing. I imagine there'll be an open verdict. You have any theories, Mr. Goldsmith?"

"I don't understand," said Goldsmith, startled.

"Well, for instance, this is off the record, of course, and just between the two of us, but I'd certainly understand if there was something you wanted to keep hushed up."

Goldsmith sipped his scotch and wondered with growing unease what the hell Vickers was talking about. An invitation to confess? With some half-hinted promise of a deal? No, he was turning bushes into bears again.

"What kind of thing would I keep hushed up, Inspector?" he asked coldly.

"You knew Mr. Housman; I didn't. Was there anything in his affairs, or his character, which might have suggested the possibility of suicide to you?"

"Suicide? I don't think so," said Goldsmith momentarily relieved as he saw the drift of Vickers's questioning.

"Give it a good going-over in your mind, Mr. Goldsmith," said the detective. "No one wants to say anything which would further upset Mrs. Housman, or possibly interfere with the payment of insurances, that kind of thing. But it's always good to know the truth."

He finished his drink and stood up.

"Don't say anything now. Just think about it. Your acquaintance with Mr. Housman was based on business, I take it?"

The question was casual. Perhaps too casual. All this man had was my name and my car number, thought Goldsmith. Yet he's bothered to unearth my address and to drive forty-odd miles to see me. And he knows I'm involved in local politics, so he's been asking around about me. A pound to a penny he knows where I work too.

"No," he answered. "Not business really. Just a chance acquaintance, that's all."

"Really? It was good of you to seek Mrs. Housman out on such a slight basis. Now I must be off. But think things over, Mr. Goldsmith. You never know what may come up. I'll keep in touch. Thanks for the drink."

He turned and left, with Goldsmith following as far as the front door. The sight of the detective's car made him even more determined to be circumspect in his dealings with the man. For a start it was pointing the wrong way for a vehicle just returning from a day in the Dales; and in addition it was a white Beetle like the one he had observed the previous day from his vantage point on the ridge. So much for "dropping in in passing."

For all he knew, Vickers had called earlier that day and actually broken into the cottage. Would a police officer of rank act like that? Goldsmith asked himself and answered, "Why not?" *Almost everyone was capable of almost everything*, was the sad philosophy his own experience had brought him. The function of civilized society was to limit the opportunities.

He went into the living-room, not knowing what to expect there. But instead of the feared shambles, he found evidence that in one respect at least he had been maligning Vickers.

On the mantelpiece in front of the clock was a note from Liz.

*Sorry about the window, but they told me at your work you were ill and when I came round with the nourishing broth and couldn't get an answer, I thought you might be lying in a coma or your bath, unable to move, so I broke in. Wherefore the malingering anyway? Give me a ring when you get back just to forgive, explain and reassure.*

He could feel beneath the surface flippancy the real concern. It must have taken an act of will in more ways than one to break that window and clamber into the empty cottage, particularly as the only way to reach the back was to go round the field. He wanted to sit quietly for a while and think about Vickers, but first he went to the phone and dialed Liz's number.

Her mother answered.

"How's my favourite politician?" she greeted him cheerfully. "Liz? Sorry, Bill, but she's out. Spreading the good word about your many virtues, no doubt. If you'd like to exercise a few of them, come round and keep me company till she returns."

"No, thanks. I'm rather busy tonight. Tell Liz I called, will you?"

He replaced the phone quickly. At least it seemed that Liz had been discreet about his absence. If she hadn't told her mother (and Mrs. Sewell would have been unable to resist a gibe) it was unlikely that she'd told anyone. Which meant he just needed a story which would satisfy her.

He made himself a cup of coffee and heated up a can of Irish stew. As he ate it, he thumbed through the large desk diary he kept by the telephone. Anything smaller he would have lost by now.

A busy week lay ahead. The annual party conference had started that day in Scarborough. He had been a delegate for the past three years but this year he had backed out and was contenting himself with a visit on the Friday. Jeff had been annoyed, but Goldsmith had persuaded him that he would be better employed staying at home, looking after the shop. National decisions were made at Scarborough, local decisions usually emanated from the billiards room of the local Labour Club. So he had got himself a weekful of committees. He didn't mind these. They were games of a kind. Sometimes you played for yourself, sometimes for the team. But they did require work in preparation. And of course at the end of the following week, he would go before the Selection Board. He ought to be working at that as well. His supporters like Liz and Jeff Malleson would be grafting away on his behalf. But the others had their backers too who would not be idle. He frowned as he finished his coffee. Perhaps he was in for a shock, but somehow he felt sure of selection. The problem which concerned him was not how to get it, but what to do when it was offered.

Do I want to be an MP? he wondered for the hundredth time. This Housman business had to be sorted out one way or another before he could answer that.

But carefully. *Parliamentary candidate arrested* was not a headline which would launch him on a rapid voyage to the Cabinet. Vickers's evident interest did at least free him from the worry of arousing it. Another visit to Sheffield was necessary. But first, that Leeds address that Simpson had given him.

He took out his street map of the city and tracked down Culham Gardens. He glanced at his watch. Quarter to eight. It was worth a drive just to check. Anything was better than sitting around doing nothing. He went out to the Land-Rover.

Culham Gardens turned out to be a street of Victorian terraced houses, once good solid middle-class dwellings though now generally declined into flats and boarding-houses. Goldsmith was reminded of Wath Grove, though the pendulum here was still swinging away from fashionability. The roadway was lined with lorries, obviously the main source of clientele for the lodgings. Supply seemed to exceed demand, however, as there were plenty of vacancy signs, including one propped against the net curtain of No. 26.

The fat middle-aged woman who came to the door regarded him with the natural suspicion of the landlady towards a prospective lodger till without much hope he put his question. The change was dramatic. A smile ran up her face like a tidal bore and Goldsmith found himself drawn irresistibly into the house.

"Neil Housman! George! George! Here's a friend of Neil's!"

George, a lugubrious fifty-year-old, seemed less enthusiastic or at least less demonstrative than his wife, who made Goldsmith sit down in the parlour and launched into a series of affectionate reminiscences of Housman. Her method was anecdotal, esoteric and digressive, but the facts which emerged were that Housman had lodged there in 1945, that he had remained there till 1949, that he had visited there from time to time in the first few years thereafter, partly because of his friendship with the Waterfields (Agnes and George) and partly because he used the house as a *poste restante* depot. But in the early 'fifties they had lost contact.

Christmas and birthday cards with no return address arrived for a while, then they too failed.

Goldsmith, posing once more as the army friend trying to get in touch, tried to turn the conversation to Housman's antecedents, but without success. He had been in the army, that was all they knew. Got one in the throat, said George. Spoke funny. Not funny, protested Agnes. Deep. Mysterious. She implied, sexy.

His civilian job in Leeds seemed equally mysterious, though Agnes remembered that he had inherited some money early on in his stay there.

All told, it did not seem like being a very profitable visit. Again and again Goldsmith was finding himself forced back on the thought that the best he could hope to find was nothing. Once again he had succeeded, but it was a frustrating business for all that.

The fat woman chattered nostalgically all the way to the door. At least Housman had been liked here, that much was evident.

"Sorry I can't help more," she said finally. "I'd like to know myself where he got to."

She eyed Goldsmith assessingly, decided he could be trusted and whispered, "There was some bother, I think."

"Bother?"

"Yes. Not long after he left a policeman came round, asking about him. Of course, I said nothing and I told Neil next time I saw him. He didn't say what it was all about, but he didn't come round so much after that. Then he didn't come at all. Still, that's life, isn't it? Ships that pass, ships that pass."

The front door opened and a well-built blonde girl of sixteen or seventeen came in and squeezed past them without comment. She reminded Goldsmith of someone.

"My daughter, Rita," said Mrs. Waterfield, noting the movement of Goldsmith's eyes.

It wasn't till he was driving away from the house that Goldsmith identified the resemblance.

Dora, Housman's girl, whom he had met the previous Saturday.

He smiled. It was perhaps the first time anything about this business had made him smile.

Obviously some ships passed closer than others.

Liz was waiting for him outside the cottage, leaning up against her Mini, smoking a cigarette. As usual she looked as if she had dressed and combed her hair while fleeing from a fire.

"You should have waited inside," he said drily, thinking of the broken window.

It was the wrong thing to say. For some time Liz had been hinting how useful it would be for her to have a key, but Goldsmith had steadfastly ignored her. At times it was true that the cold emptiness of the place could be daunting in anticipation, but at least it was a certainty. With a spare key in circulation, he could never be sure that Liz would not be waiting inside when he returned. Or Mrs. Sewell even.

"I was worried," said Liz in a hurt voice as he ushered her into the living-room. "Where the hell were you anyway? They said you were sick."

"I was," said Goldsmith. "I felt better later on, fancied some fresh air. That was all."

"Oh," she said casually. "Were you out for long?"

He was being gently investigated, he realized. Perhaps Vickers had primed his defence mechanism.

"I'm not really sure."

"Well, you picked a good day for a walk. I thought you'd changed your mind and gone to Scarborough."

She must have noticed the Land-Rover had gone. Or made it her business to check. He grunted neutrally, annoyed at having to play the question-answer game with Liz, and went into the kitchen to make some coffee. When he returned she was tidying up.

"This place could do with a good clean," she said.

"It does me."

"And you're beginning to look a bit scruffy yourself, Bill. When did you last have that jacket cleaned? And for Christ's sake get a haircut before the Selection Board. That mop doesn't suit your anti-intellectual image."

"That's what I've got, is it? Shall I work a bit of dialect into my answers?"

She took her coffee and sat down in front of the empty fireplace. The chill of autumn was in the room and the uncurtained window looking out on to the dark garden and black line of the stony ridge beyond was like a hole in space, giving a glimpse of some alien landscape. Shivering, she put down her coffee cup, rose and drew the curtains.

"Jeff wants to see you before Wednesday's meeting," she said, resuming her seat. "I expect he'll ring. You *are* well enough to go back to work tomorrow, aren't you?"

"I should think so. My *walk* did me good," he answered calmly, meeting her irony with his own. She ignored it.

"I've often wondered what made you start with politics in the first place, Bill," she said. "It struck me just the other day how little I know about you really. It's what? nine, ten years since I first met you. But before that, well you're just a blank."

"Surely not," he said lightly. "There are plenty of people round here who've known me longer than that. You must have had a nice gossip with some of them. And you know I was in the Army."

"So they say. But you never talk about the past. I don't really know what you did, where you've been, who you met. What kind of child were you? I've never met any of your ancient relatives who'll tell me embarrassing stories about your infant habits or show me old snapshots."

"That's what comes of dedicating your life to the pursuit of loneliness," he answered with a forced laugh.

"Does it? Well, when you're Prime Minister the papers will want the full biography bit. I'll just wait till then, shall I?"

Now Goldsmith laughed properly.

"Liz, behind every great man there's a great woman, they say. Now either you've got the wrong man or you're going to have to slow down a hell of a lot to get behind me!"

"You're wrong," said Liz, finishing her coffee and standing up. "You need no one behind you. That's your big asset, Bill. You look so self-contained, people believe you can do anything."

"Perhaps I can," said Goldsmith.

He did not suggest that she should stay the night, nor did she indicate if she wanted to. But as she left, she removed the coat which he'd draped carelessly over the banister at the foot of the stairs and hung it neatly on a coat-hook behind the door, as though establishing some kind of bridgehead on his territory.

# CHAPTER XI

THE FOLLOWING SATURDAY was a day of drenching showers and gusting winds. With the clouds scudding behind its tall chimney-stacks and the shrubbery boiling around its walls, Greenmansion this morning looked as if it had weighed anchor and nosed out of harbour into the open sea.

The garden looked a little less well kept than the previous week, thought Goldsmith as he drove the Land-Rover through the gates. Perhaps it was just the weather.

There were two cars parked outside the house and one of them started up as he approached and headed down the gravel drive towards him.

Goldsmith applied his brake, feeling annoyed. The drive was narrow and one of them would have to back. In addition he hoped it wasn't Mrs. Housman going out for the day. Or Vickers either. He had little desire to meet Vickers here once more.

But the car was too opulent for an honest policeman. It halted bumper to bumper with the Land-Rover and its driver got out and trotted through the rain to Goldsmith's passenger door.

It was Templewood.

"Christ almighty, what do you think you're doing here?" he demanded without ceremony, climbing in and slamming the door.

"Visiting. What about you? Selling brushes, is it?"

"I've been doing what I said I'd do," said Templewood, lighting a cigarette. "Checking up. I introduced myself as an old business friend of Housman's."

"Great minds," said Goldsmith.

"Not you too! For God's sake, forget it, Billy boy."

"Why?"

"Well, for a start, you haven't got the background, have you? Like I told you, my company has in fact done business with J. T. Hardy's, so I know the right names to drop. Also, when it comes to getting info from broken-hearted widows, some people think I'm top of the class."

He smiled smugly at Goldsmith and waggled his bushy eyebrows with a self-satisfaction that was not altogether caricature. Goldsmith stared back at him expressionlessly, the only effective counter he had ever discovered to the man's sexual vanity.

"And have you made any progress?" he asked finally.

"Give us a chance, mate!" protested Templewood. "This isn't just a bed job, is it? Not that I'd mind. No, this needs just a touch more subtlety."

"Which I lack?"

"Oh bollocks, Billy. I didn't say that! But look, it's daft to have two of us pussyfooting around here, isn't it? The last thing we want is to stir things up."

"It's a bit late," began Goldsmith, but stopped as he became aware of a blurred face outside the steamed-up passenger window.

Templewood turned and wound down the glass.

"Hello there!" he said. Outside, looking very wet, was Dora.

"Washing your hair, are you?" continued Templewood, reaching out and tugging at a rain-matted strand.

Dora smiled widely and Goldsmith suddenly felt jealous. Without the ocular proof, you could always assure yourself that ninety per cent of Templewood's instant feminine conquests were mere fantasy. But Dora's smile was genuine and affectionate.

"You said you'd look at the gears on my bike," she said accusingly. She was a very different girl from the solemn imitation-adult Goldsmith had met. Templewood's creaking charm had worked wonders in a single meeting.

"So I did, and so I shall. Instantly. See you in the garage, shall I?"

"Yes," said Dora. As she stepped back from the window, her gaze went past Templewood and met Goldsmith's for the first time.

"Oh, hello, Mr. Goldsmith," she said as she moved away.

Well, she remembered my name, thought Goldsmith, absurdly pleased, which was more than Templewood was.

"How the hell does she know your name?" he demanded.

"I was about to tell you," answered Goldsmith calmly. "I was here last week."

"Last week! Jesus! So that was you."

"I'm sorry."

"Mrs. Housman mentioned that someone had dropped in, someone else she didn't know, I mean. Well, well, Billy. Surprise. You're the fast worker when you want, aren't you? Did you get anything?"

"Not much here."

Briefly Goldsmith filled his companion in on his investigations.

"All negative, I'm afraid," he concluded.

Templewood whistled admiringly.

"You've done well, Billy boy. Only, be careful not to stir things up too much, eh? Remember, there could be a murder charge at the end of this. Or manslaughter anyway. I've not been idle myself, mind you. There's been a lot of speculation in local business circles as you'd expect, and I've been chatting up my contacts like mad. I've spent a fortune on double gins. Mind you, it has its compensations. One of the directors of J. T. Hardy's has got this wife. Christ, what a length of leg! You need to be a steeplejack! I've got half a suspicion Housman may have done a bit of climbing there himself. We shall see. You never know, he might have been gabby in bed. But so far everything in Sheffield stops or rather starts in 1950. And you've got further back than that. What was that address in Leeds again? Agnes Waterfield sounds like one for me, eh?''

Goldsmith dictated the address, then suggested they should sort out their cars before everyone in the neighbourhood noticed this encounter. He could see that Templewood was still worried in case his visit to the house should stir suspicion in Mrs. Housman's mind, but he had to agree that for Goldsmith to leave now, especially since Dora had seen him, would be very odd.

"I'll back up then," said Templewood finally. "I've got to fix the kid's bike anyway. Take care now, son. And make this your last visit. If the police are still sniffing around, it's not worth taking chances."

Goldsmith watched him reverse away with mixed feelings. Templewood's patronizing self-assurance always made him angry, but at the same time he had to admit he had misjudged the man after their meeting in the White Rose when he had been certain that his promises of help were placebos prescribed out of self-concern. Now here he was, actively and visibly engaged in the hunt for Hebbel.

As he stepped out of the Land-Rover and walked up the steps to the front door, he saw Templewood and Dora disappear into the garage together. He stared gloomily after them, thinking that if Templewood went into politics, he might indeed have some of the qualities necessary to get to Downing Street, principally charm without involvement and vanity without doubts.

"Hello, Mr. Goldsmith. How nice to see you again."

It was the high clear voice of Mrs. Housman who once again had managed to materialize unnoticed behind him. She had opened the front door to let a man out. He was of medium build, fair-haired with a bald patch like a monk's tonsure, and he had a long, set, rather awry face as though he had been eating a large mouthful of nougat and had been petrified in mid-chew. There was something vaguely familiar about him, but despite the fact that the man stared with open interest at Goldsmith, Mrs. Housman made no attempt to introduce the two.

"Please step inside, Mr. Goldsmith. I won't be a moment."

He obeyed, glad to get out of range of the man's scrutiny. He could be another policeman, perhaps, but Templewood would surely have warned him of his presence. If he had known.

"Good day, Mr. Munro," he heard the woman say. Then she came through the door and closed it behind her.

She was a very attractive woman. He found himself contrasting her small, delicate features and cool self-possession with Liz's much greater exuberance of both appearance and personality. This one might not trudge from door to door canvassing in a rain-storm, but she would know how to send her husband's dinner guests home convinced that their host was a man with a future.

"I'm sorry to intrude again," he began awkwardly as she led him into the same room as on the previous occasion.

"It's no intrusion. I'm delighted you were able to return so soon. And this time you mustn't rush off so quickly. Would you like some coffee? I've just made some. Or a drink perhaps?"

"No, it's a little early for me. Coffee would be fine."

She looked much more relaxed than she had done the previous week. Most of the lines of tension had left her face. Perhaps, thought Goldsmith suddenly, Templewood had offered to tickle her breasts with his eye-brows.

The thought made him feel guilty, as if he'd spoken it aloud. No, he decided, watching her pour the coffee with an economic grace of movement, she's not his type. The Templewood tactics would have little effect here.

"How's your little girl?" he asked.

"I think she's over the worst," she replied, glancing at her wrist-watch. "She should be home soon. She insisted on going to the shops despite the rain. It's my birthday on Monday, so it all had to be done secretly and by herself."

She smiled with a kind of rueful affection as she spoke.

"She is back," said Goldsmith. "I saw her by the garage."

"Oh good. She'll be pleased to see you again."

It was mere politeness, Goldsmith knew, yet the idea gave him a disproportionate pleasure. He recognized that he would have to watch this carefully and not forget the real and squalid basis of his relationship with this family.

Mrs. Housman's next remark did the reminding for him, putting him on full alert.

"Forgive my asking, Mr. Goldsmith, but my husband did not owe you money by any chance, did he?"

"No!" he said strongly. "What gave you such an idea?"

"Well, it's always a possibility that undocumented debts are left, isn't it? And the embarrassment of mentioning them must be acute. Neil tended to emulate the Gulbenkians and Gettys of the world and carry little or no cash with him, I know. So I thought . . ."

She let her voice tail off in a beautifully modulated dying fall.

I'm being offered an option, thought Goldsmith suddenly. Look sheepish, say *well, yes, as a matter of fact it was just fifty, seventy-five, a hundred pounds . . .* and the cheque-book would come out. I would finish my coffee and she would smile sweetly and offer her hand as I left. For good.

"I think Inspector Vickers must have been talking to you," he said.

"Really? Why?"

"Probably uttering warning words about strange men scavenging round the tables of rich funeral feasts."

She smiled sweetly now, but with genuine sweetness.

"He may have said something. Let me apologize if I've offended you, but it seemed simpler to speak directly. I'm glad I was wrong."

"Of course, I could be after larger game," said

Goldsmith boldly and to his own amazement. This was Templewood's line, not his!

"That I can deal with without the police. Let's talk about Neil, shall we?"

"Of course. I'm sorry. You were his secretary, weren't you, before you married?"

"He told you that?"

"He must have done," he answered.

"Interesting. You must have been close to him. He talked very little of personal matters to others. He never mentioned you to me, for example. Yes, I was his secretary. I'd been working as a typist at Hardy's for about a year when he joined the firm. I was his secretary for only two or three months. He offered me the job himself, asked me to go out after a fortnight, asked me to marry him six weeks later. A whirlwind romance, I think they call it."

"You must have made a strong impression," said Goldsmith. "Neil struck me as a thoughtful, prepared kind of man. Most things he did would get careful advanced planning."

"Yes," said Mrs. Housman neutrally.

And *yes*, thought Goldsmith. She wondered herself now. Thirteen years of marriage must have made her wonder. Was Housman the kind of man to be swept off his feet? Or the kind of man to see in this woman something that he needed? Nothing as blatant as being the boss's daughter or related to the county gentry, but qualities of composure, dignity and reliability which would give impetus to and weather with an ambitious man's rise. And was it too fanciful to think that these qualities were all the better for being found in a girl young enough to be swept off *her* feet into an unquestioning acceptance of the relationship for many years?

Fanciful or not, the questions must eventually have come. The point was, did any answers follow?

"Dora must have been born fairly early in your marriage," he said.

"Yes. Not too early," she said, with a gentle ironic stress.

"No, of course not," he said quickly.

"That doesn't follow either," she said.

Goldsmith began to feel he was being quietly mocked.

"It must have been fascinating to know Neil in those early days with Hardy's," he said. "Before he built it up from nothing."

"Hardly nothing, Mr. Goldsmith. It was a good sound business in a small way; just beginning to flourish again after the war. A good injection of capital was all that was needed. And a bit of know-how about cutting corners on building regulations and getting hold of materials. That's what Neil brought to Hardy's."

"Which?" asked Goldsmith. "The know-how or the capital?"

"Both."

"Useful. Where did he get it, I wonder?"

"Which?"

"Either."

She looked at him assessingly, mocking no longer. She's wondering what I'm all about, thought Goldsmith. She senses this isn't a real, normal, inconsequential conversation, but for the life of her, she can't guess what it really is. Can she?

"As far as money goes," said Mrs. Housman slowly, "I think Neil inherited quite a lot from his parents. They died at the end of the war."

How much was *quite a lot*? Goldsmith remembered the little shop. Its value in 1945 couldn't have been more than a few hundred pounds. Some stock; goodwill; say an equivalent amount stashed away in savings over the years; insurances; did that come to *quite a lot*?

Templewood would know how to find out how much Housman had in fact put into the company. He made a mental note to mention this to him next time they talked.

"And the know-how?" he said. "Neil never mentioned any kind of formal training he'd had."

"I don't think they run courses in that kind of thing," she answered. The mockery was back. It was as if she were inviting him to discover that the marriage had been unhappy, that she had held her husband in low

esteem. Perhaps the tight mask of self-control she
wore covered not deep grief but total indifference. He
wondered how much difference it would make to his
nights if he could believe that this woman had not
found her widowing as tragic as it seemed. It was a
line worth pursuing. This hunt for Hebbel was after all
in part merely a hunt for heart's ease.

"It's stopped raining, I think," she said casually, as
if deciding the journey into the past had gone far
enough.

"So it has," said Goldsmith, looking towards the
window but seeing no farther than the pustules of rain
on the glass. He must make an effort at a bit of small
talk, he thought; let the information come incidentally
rather than conduct an inquisition.

"You have a lovely house," was the best he could
manage.

"Thank you. Would you like to see it?" she asked.

"Why, yes."

"I'll give you the conducted tour then. It will be a
good rehearsal."

She rose and led him to the door.

"Rehearsal for what? You're not going to sell, are
you?"

"Perhaps. Upstairs first, I think. That way you don't
have to take prospective buyers through any room
more than once. That's the technique, isn't it? Let
them see but not inspect."

"I wouldn't know. I've never sold a house."

"Lucky you. Are you married, Mr. Goldsmith?"

"No."

Briefly he gave her an account of his working background and described his cottage. If Vickers had all
the facts, there seemed no reason why she should not
be as well informed.

"It sounds lonely," was her comment.

"It is sometimes. But that's what it's all about, isn't
it?"

"Observe the balustrade on this staircase," she said.
"Handcarved by local craftsmen, I believe. Two at
least. The style is intermittent. The landing is light,

airy and extensive, which is one way of saying that curtains and carpets will cost a fortune. This is the master bedroom."

It was a large room. Goldsmith didn't like the proportions which to his mind were not quite right. The room did not fit him, somehow. Perhaps it was too feminine. But it was a fine room for all that, decorated with quiet and expensive good taste. Goldsmith found his gaze being drawn to the huge bed which was draped with a coverlet made by stitching together the pelts of some small brown and white animal. It struck a jarring but curiously sensual note. It disturbed him, and for diversion he picked up a small primitively stylized wood-carving of a woman which stood on the dressing-table.

"Are you interested in art?" asked Mrs. Housman politely.

"I know what I like," he answered, deliberately stressing his Northern vowels. He was rewarded with a smile.

"Neil brought it back from one of his trips. It's South American Indian, I believe."

Goldsmith felt his pulse move into a higher gear.

"Yes, I believe he mentioned he'd been to Peru," he said. "I remember telling him there wouldn't be much work for a Yorkshire builder there."

"It was a matter of investment, not building," said Mrs. Housman. "My husband liked to make money work for him, and for the business. He was willing to speculate, but he liked to see what he was putting his cash into. I believe there was some mining venture in Peru which an old army friend was connected with."

"I hope it was profitable."

"For a while, but I think after his second visit he had doubts and decided to pull out. I won't know till his affairs have been fully sorted out. Shall we continue the tour?"

He followed her out of the bedroom. It had been easy. Too easy, perhaps, whatever that meant. Would she have found a way to volunteer the information about Peru even if he had not picked up the wood-

sculpture? No, that was absurd. It would mean that
(a) she knew her husband was Hebbel and (b) she
knew that he was on his trail. Could that be possible?
He doubted it. Or at least he did not want to believe
it.

He peered politely into bathrooms, guest-rooms and
box-rooms. It was a straightforward, rather dull house,
much more interesting externally than inside. He recalled the line of dormer windows and asked, "You
have another floor?"

"Yes," she said. "Would you like to see?"

"It could be a selling point," he said.

A door tucked away at the end of the landing led to
a continuation on a more modest scale of the main
stair-case.

"Dora has her room up here, by choice, and she's
laid claim to most of the other space," said Mrs.
Housman. "Something romantic about a room under
the eaves, I think. She dislikes right-angles. Here we
are."

She pushed open a door and stood aside, Goldsmith
was reluctant to enter.

"Should we?" he said.

"Children are entitled to privacy," she agreed. "They
are also entitled to know that privacy can and will be
invaded."

As they entered, a telephone rang distantly.

"Have a look around," said the woman. "I won't be
a moment."

This room was much more to Goldsmith's liking.
The roof sloped sharply enough to avoid the sense of
enclosure he often felt in attic rooms, and in any case
this room ran almost half the length of the house and
incorporated four of the dormers. Each of the alcoves
had been decorated with different wall-paper, one with
an exotic, intertwining plant motif, another with a
pattern of old grey stones, the third with pseudo-
paneling and the fourth with plain white. The wall
opposite the windows had a modern, bright design on
it. Jazzy was the old word which came to Goldsmith's
mind. A huge doll's house was pushed against it. The

wall against which Dora's bed stood had once been white too, but now it was covered with hand prints in various colours with names (presumably of their owners) beneath them. And the fourth wall was invisible behind an interlocking combination of wardrobe, dressing-table, book-case and cupboards.

If you wanted to spend a lot of money on kids, he thought, a room like this seemed a pretty sensible way of spending it.

He thought he heard a floorboard creak outside the door and turned to face it, determined that the Housman silent entrance was not going to disconcert him this time.

"Hello," said Dora. She was still wearing her damp rain-coat and seemed neither surprised nor annoyed at finding him there.

"I'm sorry if I'm trespassing," he said, "but your mother . . ."

"That's all right. I heard her. I've been waiting till she went."

The girl produced a small oblong package in shop gift-wrapping from her pocket and looked assessingly round the room, explaining, "It's Mummy's birthday on Monday and I want to hide her present."

"That shouldn't be hard," he said. "I mean, she's not likely to come looking for it!"

"She brought you up here," replied Dora. It was a mere statement of fact, not a reproach.

She took hold of the doll's house and pulled. It was on castors and slid easily away from the wall, revealing a small disused fireplace, presumably the sole source of warmth for the household servant who had inhabited the attic originally.

"Daddy wanted to fill it in, but it's my secret hiding-place," Dora explained, depositing her packet in the grate and pushing the house back against the wall.

Goldsmith felt flattered at being so readily let into the girl's secret.

"I like your room," he said. "Was the decoration your idea?"

"Partly," she said, taking off her raincoat. "The

windows were Daddy's, though. See, they're all different and when I sit in the recesses, I can imagine I'm in different places. Look."

She went to the one with the vegetable design.

"Here I'm in a tree house in the jungle. Somewhere where you watch the animals coming to drink. Like Tree Tops in Africa."

"Have you been there?"

"No, but Daddy promised to take me when I was fifteen. This one with the paneling is a very old house and I can be a princess or something like that watching an army going off to war. The stone one is a dungeon. I'm a prisoner, wondering if my friends have forgotten me."

"And the white one."

"That can be anything I like. A hospital sometimes. Or an igloo. Or an aeroplane. Do you like my hands?"

She was referring to the prints on the wall over her bed, Goldsmith realized.

"Yes. Are they to keep the spirits away?"

"Pardon?"

"Somewhere, in the East I think, they do that as a protection against spirits. That's what I read, anyway."

"No," she said reluctantly. "It wasn't for that. Just my friends' prints. Would you like to put yours up?"

"Why, thank you," said Goldsmith.

But before he could be initiated into the circle of hand-printers, Mrs. Housman returned.

"There you are, Dora," she said. "Don't forget we're going out to lunch. I want to leave in about ten minutes. Mr. Wilson wants me to call in his office on the way."

"But Mr. Goldsmith is going to do a hand-print," protested the girl.

"Another time perhaps. Mr. Goldsmith's hands won't change."

The girl looked disappointed, Goldsmith shrugged helplessly at her.

"Why don't you come to Mummy's birthday tea?" she suggested suddenly. "I'm baking a cake at school."

"Mr. Goldsmith has a job to do, Dora," said Mrs. Housman.

"Thank you very much," said Goldsmith. "I don't know if I can get away, you see. But I would have liked very much to come."

"Ten minutes, Dora," said Mrs. Housman, leading him from the room.

"I'm sorry to hurry you," she said as they descended the stairs. "Wilson's my solicitor and there's some matter he wants to talk to me about. If it's urgent enough for him to ring on a Saturday morning, then it must be fairly important. Please come again, Mr. Goldsmith."

"I'd like to," he said.

She offered him her hand, small-boned, delicate. Her close-cut black hair picked up the watery sunlight as she opened the front door, and for a moment a thin aureole gleamed round her head. She was a figure of striking beauty.

Goldsmith glanced up as he climbed into the Land-Rover. Dora was standing in one of her alcoves. He waved. She didn't wave back, but he felt she was watching him.

As he drove away he tried to work out which of the alcoves she had chosen, but found it impossible.

# CHAPTER XII

On Sunday Goldsmith once again ducked the Sewells' telephoned invitation to lunch, pleading that he had a great deal of work to get through.

This was in fact true and Liz, having already expressed concern that recently he had appeared to be marking time in his political progress, had to accept the excuse. But she extracted from him a promise to come round for a substantial supper that evening.

There was a considerable backlog of minutes to be read, letters to be written, proposals to be drafted, telephone calls to be made, and by eight-thirty, Goldsmith was very ready to leave it all behind him. He stopped at the pub to pick up a few bottles of beer.

"Haven't seen much of you this week," said the landlord, a rather dour Yorkshireman whose barmanship stopped at drawing pints. Even shandy he considered a frivolously complicated drink which must be southern in origin.

"I've been busy, Len," said Goldsmith. "Have you missed me then?"

"No, but some has."

"Really?"

"Aye. There was a fellow asking about you last Sunday after you'd left. Had a white car."

"Was there now?" Vickers, guessed Goldsmith.

"And this lunchtime again."

"Same fellow?"

"No. Another. Same type though. Are you going to pay for them beers or are you collecting for charity?"

"Sorry," said Goldsmith, passing over the money.

110

Another policeman? he wondered. He did not like the feel of this.

As he turned from the bar, Cyril Fell the builder entered. There was no way of avoiding him and Goldsmith steeled himself for another bout of complaint and accusation aimed at his fellow councillors. But it didn't come. Fell hardly glanced at him, gave him a minimal nod and headed for the far end of the bar.

Relieved, but also puzzled, Goldsmith drove to Liz's. Perhaps Fell had sought a sympathetic ear elsewhere. In any case, more disturbing at the moment was the thought that the police might still be investigating him. He had hoped to find a chance of asking Mrs. Housman about the progress of the official investigation of her husband's death, but the opportunity had not arisen.

Mrs. Sewell opened the front door for him. She had a drink in her hand and a great deal more in her belly.

"Hello, stranger," she said. "Don't I get a kiss? It's been a long time."

He pecked her cheek and ducked beneath the arm she tried to drape round his neck.

"Where's Liz?" he asked.

"They're in there, plotting the fucking revolution as usual."

She was far gone. Swearing occupied a high point on her alcoholic curve.

"They?" asked Goldsmith, taking off his coat.

"She and Malleson. You've been a naughty boy. Going to get a hundred lines."

"I've been writing them all day," said Goldsmith, annoyed that his supper was going to be turned into a work session.

He went through into the living-room.

"Hello, Liz. Jeff," he said.

"Bill, you skipped ward surgery again yesterday morning," said Malleson.

"Hardly skipped. I got Johnson to stand in for me."

"It's not the point, Bill. Things get noticed, you'd be surprised. And this is just the time when you should be seen out and about, making friends and influencing people."

"I thought I had friends," said Goldsmith. Part of his mind recognized that Malleson was right to rebuke him, but another, stronger part was bent on being as unco-operative and obstreperous as possible. Perhaps I'm jealous, he thought, glancing at Liz who was sitting next to Malleson on the sofa, looking anxious and puzzled. And untidy. Why couldn't she spend a bit of time on herself?

"You have," said Malleson. "And they're working a bit harder for you at the moment than you seem to care to do for yourself."

"Come on, Jeff! So I miss a Saturday morning. I have business of my own, a private life too."

"Two Saturdays," insisted Malleson. "Next, you cry off the Conference, then you're supposed to be ill on Monday, yet no one can find you at home."

Goldsmith looked angrily at Liz who flushed but did not look away. Malleson had not finished.

"A couple of weeks ago you took off two days early for your reunion, and you seem to have been in bottom gear ever since."

"You said I made a good impression on Edmunds and Barraclough when I spoke at the ward meeting," said Goldsmith, trying to maintain things at the argument level.

"That was speaking, not working."

"Was it? Well, today I've been working and I feel precious little like speaking. I came to eat and if I stay it'll be just to eat. Nothing more!"

As soon as he said this he saw that Liz had misinterpreted it.

"That's all you were invited for," she snapped, standing up. "Though you seem to think you're doing us a bloody great favour by coming at all."

"For Christ's sake! Who said anything about favours?" he retorted angrily. "You want me to come, I come. You want me to go, I'll go. It's that simple!"

"Bill, this isn't like you," began Liz.

"No, it's like a spoilt four-year-old," interjected Malleson. "This is serious business we're doing. There's no place for tantrums."

"No? Then if it's so serious, Jeff, you'd better do it yourself, you're such a serious person. *You* go before the selection board and see if they'll pick *you!*"

It was an unpleasant gibe. Malleson's own political ambitions had once been large, but several unsuccessful attempts to secure a nomination had made him an object of ridicule in some quarters.

"At least they'd get someone reliable," he retorted.

"Perhaps. But would they know they'd got anyone at all?"

It was a good exit line and Mrs. Sewell standing in the doorway listening with wide-eyed enjoyment tucked her glass under her arm and applauded vigorously as Goldsmith pushed by her.

"Bill!" called Liz as he opened the front door. He looked back. She was standing alongside her mother.

"Don't go," said Liz.

He hesitated on the threshold. Mrs. Sewell stretched out her plump arms towards him.

"Come to Mummy," she said throatily.

He slammed the door behind him and within seconds was doing an illegal fifty mph through the empty streets.

It was, he knew, absurd, though in a way it had been positively enjoyable. It had been years since he had engaged in such a splendidly childish argument and at the same time as he deplored what he had said, his mind was working out better, more elegantly phrased gibes he might have used.

He had left the street lights behind him now and he made himself concentrate on his driving. The wet gusty weather of the previous morning had returned. Flurries of rain were hurled at his windscreen and, high above, the athletic wind was tearing holes in the thick cloud cover. But it was a moonless night and the scraps of star-pricked sky that momentarily appeared offered no lumination. The familiar road seemed looped and knotted and he slowed down even further. No agument, especially one so uncertainly based and inelegantly pursued, was worth getting killed for. Survival rated high in his priorities.

He was relieved to see the black outline of the cottage. As she bumped the Land-Rover up the kerb, the windows threw back the headlight beam for a second before he switched off. And there was another flicker from an upstairs window, just for the briefest of moments and so quick he might have been mistaken. But if someone with a shaded torch, suddenly disturbed by the light from the vehicle, had turned quickly and switched off the torch too late, it might have looked like that.

Goldsmith jumped out of the Land-Rover and rushed to his front door. His key was in the hole and turned with the speed and accuracy of years. But the door didn't budge. Someone had slid the bolts home inside.

He stooped to the letter box and pushed it open. A shadowy figure was moving with haste but without panic down the passage into the kitchen. Goldsmith remembered the broken window which he had merely patched with a piece of cardboard. This was one burglar who had had things easy.

There was no direct way round the side of the cottage. Presumably the intruder had worked this out too. Goldsmith ran back to the Land-Rover, clambered on the bonnet, stepped from here to the roof of the single-story wash-house and store-room which blocked off access at the right-hand side of the cottage and scrambled along the sloping slippery tiles. He went as fast as he could with little concern for his own safety or the state of repair of the roof. But there was no way to be fast enough, and when he reached a point from which he could see into the back garden, it was empty. Then through the apple trees, his straining eyes saw a movement on top of the wall which separated his property from the sloping field beyond. Someone had just passed over it, and even at this distance and in this darkness the impression Goldsmith got once more was one of careful, unflurried movement.

Goldsmith was more enraged by this than by the idea of the break-in itself. Pursuit was useless. The man had too great a start and all directions to choose from. The logical thing was to get into the house, inspect the damage, ring the police. No; not from here anyway. This fellow would almost certainly have disconnected the phone. He moved as if he knew all the answers. Only Goldsmith's unforecastably early return had caught him unawares.

He scrambled back along the wash-house roof panting from his exertions, his brain working coldly, calculatingly. His visitor was not alone in being able to forecast reactions. He had to have a car and it must be close. The most likely place was in the lane which ran over the ridge, across the ford to the farm-house at the other side of the valley. From here all he would have had to do was clamber over the stone wall and make his way across the field behind the cottage.

A hypothesis is nothing unless it's tested, thought Goldsmith as he climbed into the Land-Rover, switched on and reversed into the road at a speed which did not allow for the possibility of other traffic. The vehicle's acceleration was not one of its welling points and he was still far from top speed when he had to start slowing down to take the corner into the lane. He almost didn't make it, slipping sideways in the beginnings of a four-wheel skid on the wet tarmac, but this was something the Land-Rover *was* well equipped to deal with; and the tractor-etched ruts of the lane's surface, which the rain was rapidly turning into twin rivers, offered no problems at all.

His headlights were on full beam—there was no point in attempting a stealthy approach—and by the time he had travelled three hundred yards, he began to suspect he was wrong. The lane ran arrow straight to the crest of the ridge and clearly no car was parked on this side of it. There was no reason he could think of for his burglar to have left his car farther than this. He would have needed some light to manoeuvre the vehicle round and would not have wanted to risk attracting attention from the farm-house.

Goldsmith slowed down, swearing softly. The line between hypothesis and credo was always very narrow and easily crossed unawares. It was difficult to rethink the situation, and probably it was far too late. Ahead

on his right was a gateway through the wall where he
would be able to turn. He pulled the wheel round and
ran the bonnet up against the gate, prior to getting out
and opening it. Then he noticed that the cast-iron
hoop by which the gate was fastened to the wall-end
was not in place. Even as his mind worked out the
possible implications of this, his hand thrust the gear
lever forward, his foot stamped down on the accelerator and the Land-Rover's bumper hit the bottom bar
of the gate and sent it swinging madly open. A figure
started from behind the wall. A few yards away up the
hill and parked snugly out of sight against the wall was
a Mini. The man, anonymously bulky in a plastic
raincoat, gum boots and broad-rimmed hat, instinctively headed for the car.

If he gets into it, I've got him, thought Goldsmith
triumphantly as he put the gears into four-wheel drive
and swung the wheel hard over. There was no way in
which a Mini could get away from a Land-Rover in
these conditions.

But his burglar was a thinker. Hiding the car in the
field in case anyone legitimately using the farm-track
should notice it, had been the work of a thoughtful
man. Now he turned from the Mini to face the oncom-
ing Land-Rover, raising his hands to his face as he did
so.

A gesture of surrender? wondered Goldsmith. Or
just concealment? He wants to conceal his identity
which could mean I know him and which must mean
he still hopes to get away!

The man broke and ran straight at the Land-Rover,
side-stepping left at the last moment and heading
straight down the hill. It took a few seconds for Goldsmith to reverse and by the time he had done so, his
burglar had a thirty-yard start. Angrily he stamped
hard on the accelerator and rapidly bore down on the
fleeing figure. The fool had no hope of reaching the
bottom of the field before he was overtaken. He glanced
over his shoulder; in panic, thought Goldsmith. But
there was no panic in the way in which he stopped,
turned again and flung himself sideways out of the line

of the fast-moving Land-Rover. Even that vehicle's versatility provided no quick way of stopping at fifty mph, on a soft, sodden grassy slope.

In fact, thought Goldsmith, his anger suddenly gone, it might not prove too difficult to turn the thing over if you really put your mind to it and tried to turn *and* decelerate at the same time.

By the time he had arranged his movements in a non-fatal order, the burglar was back at his Mini. If it had started first time, that would have been an end of the matter. But the rain or perhaps some untypical hastiness on the driver's part interfered. The starter roared, the engine turned, almost caught, then wheezed to silence. And again. And again.

It was at the seventh or eighth try that it started. Even then this was almost soon enough. The Mini bounded forward, swung out slightly to make room for the turn through the gateway and almost made it as the Land-Rover arrived. The best Goldsmith could do was drive hard at the little car's side. He caught it just above the rear wheel. It was only a glancing blow but strong enough to shatter the Land-Rover's left headlamp and push the Mini's back end round so that the turning circle became too tight and there was no way through the solid stone wall.

The driver did not hesitate. He grasped the situation at a glance, opened his door and scrambled out.

They were only three yards apart at this point. Goldsmith thought of getting out of the Land-Rover and meeting the man on equal terms, but the thought was only a passing one. Anyone who gave up an advantage such as he had was a fool. The other might be ten years younger, an experienced and expert brawler. The only struggle he, Goldsmith, had taken part in during the past twenty years had been that farcical, tragic last waltz with Housman which had caused all this trouble. That there was a connection between that business and this he took for granted, though what it could be was at present a total mystery. Time to think of that later. At the moment his job was to keep track

of the man in the plastic mac. He hoped that he would
try to repeat his previous down-hill manœuvre.

But the other had also learned from his failure. He
set off running once more, but this time up the ridge.
Goldsmith followed cautiously, trying to work out tactics. In the first heat of pursuit, it had seemed quite
reasonable just to run the man down. Clearly that was
out of the question. The sensible thing to do was to
concentrate on the car, immobilize it and contact the
police. They would soon track the intruder down,
probably that same night. The trouble then would be
that he would not see the man till his case came up in
court, and he wanted desperately to find out the reason for the breakin. There was always the possibility
that it was in fact a policeman he was chasing. Vickers
struck him as a man not above taking short-cuts. But
in that case what did Vickers imagine he was going to
find in the cottage? Or anyone, for that matter?

No, the thing to do was just drive this poor fellow
round and round till he dropped from exhaustion,
then have a heart-to-heart with him.

The "poor fellow," he suddenly realized, was far
from abandoning the game yet. The single headlight
was adequate for keeping him in view, but it was also
picking out the rocky outcrops and small boulders
which became more and more frequent as you approached the top of the ridge. The running man was
selecting a route which took him across and through as
many of these obstacles as possible and Goldsmith
realized his quarry was drawing away as the Land-
Rover twisted and turned to avoid the stones.

He tried to speed up; one of the front wheels bucked
violently and he heard the bottom of the vehicle rasp
along some unyielding obstruction. He swore anxiously
and slowed down again. Ahead the man had reached
the crest and was disappearing behind one of the three
lightning-struck trees which tonight were in their Gothic
element. A short while later he brought the Land-
Rover to a halt beneath their skeletal shade. Below, at
the foot of the lightly wooded slope which fell away
more sharply on this side, he could just make out a

line of more polished darkness which he knew was the little river. The farm-house beyond was almost invisible against the uncontrasting background and no lights showed. They kept early hours here still.

And nowhere on the slope below him could he see anything which vaguely resembled a man.

One thing he could not afford to do was sit and wait. His burglar might be sitting behind a tree watching him. Or he might be heading down the hill, planning to by-pass the farmhouse and cut across country to the main road five miles to the north. A good way of getting himself killed, thought Goldsmith, not without satisfaction. But this fellow had not so far struck him as being ready to get himself killed. No, his idea would still be to get back to the Mini. Even with a dent in its side, it would still be drivable, and he would know that Goldsmith had not paused to immobilize it.

That's what I should do now, thought Goldsmith. Back down the ridge, pull the innards out of that car, then go for the police.

Instead he moved the Land-Rover forward till it was on the down slope of the valley, applied the footbrake, studied the ground ahead, then switched off the engine and surviving headlight. Immediately, without waiting for the night-sight to develop, he released the footbrake and freewheeled down the slope for twenty or thirty feet. Here he applied the brake again and waited till shapes and movement began to make themselves felt through the darkness. Below him to his left was a small clump of elders. He waited till an extra gust of wind shook their thin branches, then released the brake once more and slid gently down behind their shifting protection.

With luck, his burglar would now have as little idea where his pursuer was as he had of the other's position. For a while the man would lie low, then begin moving cautiously back towards the crest of the ridge. That was part of the hypothesis. The other part was that the man would be farther down the slope than the Land-Rover was and somewhere between it and the wall. Indeed for all he knew the man had scrambled over the wall and was now walking back down the lane at his leisure. But the hypothesis did not cater for that possibility and Goldsmith put it out of his mind firmly.

He glanced down at the luminous dial of his watch. Five minutes, he had decided. The other was a careful man, would wait at least that long.

The night was as wild as ever. The three dead trees which commanded the ridge groaned and protested as the wind tore at their carbonized limbs. Always in stormy weather they suffered some diminution of stature and the morning would find them with some new grotesquerie of outline and their disjointed members lying in the grass across their surface roots.

The five minutes were up. He counted another sixty seconds then switched on the engine and his one remaining headlight at the same time.

For a moment he thought he had failed. Driving rain, swaying trees, unyielding rocks: there was nothing else to see in the white cone which lay athwart the slope.

Slowly he sent the Land-Rover moving forward. Then only a few yards ahead the man rose up from the ground and stood full in the beam.

"Now, you bastard," murmured Goldsmith, and increased his speed slightly. The man took two or three uncertain steps backwards, slipped and sank to the ground again. Goldsmith, triumphant, ran the Land-Rover towards him. His plan was to halt alongside the recumbent figure and urbanely invite him aboard for a conversation. But as the bonnet of the slowing vehicle passed the man, he pushed himself upright. In his hand was a large round rock. He swung it hard against the surviving headlight and darkness fell again.

His recent scruples forgotten, Goldsmith accelerated and swung the wheel hard over. His sole thought was to get the man and if that involved cracking a bone or two, he did not for the moment care. The Land-Rover rushed blindly forward, there may or may not have been a slight bump against the side, but almost immediatley the bonnet struck something head on which was far too solid to be a man. Goldsmith felt himself pitched forward and upward, his brow struck the windscreen, his chest the upper rim of the steering wheel and he fell sideways across the front seat.

He had no sense of losing consciousness. He felt that he had pushed himself upright almost immediately. For a moment rain, trees and broken cloud seemed to lie flat and still against the window pane. Suddenly they jerked back into perspective and motion, and when he looked at his watch more than half an hour had passed since he had sprung his ambush.

His chest ached and his forehead had a large bump on it, but nothing seemed broken. He opened the door and half-tumbled out of the Land-Rover. The wind and rain were welcome revivers and after a moment he was able to inspect the damage. He had hit a hefty sapling, bending it back so that the green and white fibres bulged through the bark like varicose veins. He had been lucky. If it had been a rock, the impact might have been much more serious, for himself as well as the vehicle. As it was, both still seemed able to function, but he had no intention of trying to get the Land-Rover back up the hill without lights.

He removed the keys, locked the door and wearily set off up the ridge towards the Gothic trees. He glanced towards the gateway in the wall as he descended on the other side and noted without surprise that the Mini had gone. It didn't matter, he told himself as he entered his cottage by the burglar's route. The man's escape was only temporary. When he had caught him in the headlight beam for the last time he had got a clear view of his face. And he knew where to start looking for him.

He did not pause to inspect the cottage for theft or damage but downed a stiff whisky, pulled off his wet clothes, fell on his bed and went to sleep.

# CHAPTER XIII

HE WAS AWOKEN by a thunderous knocking at the front door. Feeling dreadful, he went down the stairs and opened it.

"My God!" said Liz. "You look awful."

She came in uninvited and led him into the living-room.

"What's happened to you?"

"I had a bit of an accident."

"I've noticed. Let's clean you up a bit."

It was rather pleasant to relax and admit her expert ministrations. She told him she had tried to ring the previous night but had not been able to get through. Similarly this morning, and she'd decided to catch him before he set off for work.

"Last night's row was stupid," she said. "I should have realized you wanted to relax, not listen to Jeff rattling on. Mind you, you were a bit rough on him. On all of us."

"I'll apologize," he said. He had let her believe he'd had a few drinks after leaving her house, been in-volved in a slight accident and decided to abandon the Land-Rover in the interests of safety. He had been examining the living-room as he spoke, and though there were signs of a search—drawers and doors pulled open, books disturbed—there was nothing not attrib-utable to alcoholic disorderliness. Even the telephone cord might have been pulled accidentally out of its socket.

He began to feel better after coffee, aspirin and a substantial breakfast. His chest was badly bruised and he had to promise Liz he would consult a doctor before she would let him go to collect the Land-Rover. He had been deliberately vague about its whereabouts, saying it was "up the road a bit" and this seemed to satisfy her. He also expected more opposition to his declaration that he was going to work, but Liz merely nodded, said that as she had a bit of time coming, she thought she'd take the morning off and, unless he had any great objection, start putting his house to rights.

It was an opportunity she had been long awaiting, he knew, and it would have taken more churlishness than he had the strength for that morning to refuse. Her concern for him was flattering and he wondered as he had often done recently whether it was just her mother's propinquity that made it seem threatening also. He found himself comparing mother and daughter. It was not difficult, even though it might be unjust, to detect the lineaments of the older woman in the younger. He found himself considering as a foil to them both the cool, ordered, self-containment of Jennifer Housman. Even her appearance with its unobtrusively elegant grooming contrasted with the conscious flamboyance of Mrs. Sewell and with Liz's *laissez faire*.

He would have a chance of examining the contrast more closely that day when he visited Greenmansion again to make discreet inquiries about the man he had met coming out of the house on Saturday. The man called Munro. The man who had stood and faced him in the headlight's glare on the far side of the ridge last night.

As far as he had been able to check without arousing Liz's curiosity by making a formal inventory, nothing was missing from the cottage. He considered the problem as he trudged along the lane. (It would have been quicker to enter the field through his back garden, but Liz's curiosity was again the obstacle.)

Munro might have found what he was looking for. Or he might have been disturbed too soon. Or he might have been mistaken and what he was looking for just wasn't there. Like most reasoned analyses of alternatives, this one did not help at all.

Presumably Munro was the other man inquiring about him at the local. Len, the landlord, had described him as being the "same kind" as Vickers. Yet though it had been easy in the heat of the chase to accept cynically that the police were capable of anything, now in this clear washed-out morning it proved more difficult. Certainly if Munro had anything to do with the police it would look most suspicious if no report of the break-in was made.

Of course, the police might not be the only interested party. If Housman were Hebbel then he might have left friends, friends of a very peculiar nature. Goldsmith shivered. The idea was fantastic. But even the idea of receiving the attentions of a neo-Nazi group was enough to make him feel uneasy.

The Land-Rover started first time and he was able to back away from the sapling and traverse the ridge once more without trouble. The terrain this morning looked very easy and the Gothic grove on the crest had shrunk and bent into three rather pathetic dead trees.

He put the Land-Rover into the firm's repair shop, telling them not to worry about damage to the bodywork but to concentrate on getting the lamps back in working order.

The bump on his forehead ached all day and midway through the afternoon he used it as a part-genuine excuse for leaving the office early. The Land-Rover was ready, still slightly battered, but with the lights repaired, and he pointed it south towards Sheffield. He realized that so quick a return might appear curious to Mrs. Housman and there was the danger that her curiosity might be passed on to Vickers. But the trail of Munro had to be followed while it was hot. In any case the obvious motive for visiting an attractive, wealthy and recently widowed woman might easily be attributed to him.

He sampled this idea for a while and found it surprisingly distasteful. He analysed this reaction further and discovered it was caused by a reluctance to have Jennifer Houseman believe him capable of such indelicate cupidity. To his estimation in the eyes of Inspector Vickers he felt quite indifferent.

In the event, matters were made very easy for him. Dora opened the door before he could knock.

"I knew you would come," she said. "Come in, please."

Puzzled, Goldsmith followed her into the house.

"Walk this way, please," she said over her shoulder, adding, "There's a joke. I just mean 'follow me' but you might imitate the way I'm walking if you wanted."

"Oh, I see," said Goldsmith laughing, not too artificially he hoped.

Mrs. Housman was sitting in the lounge. On a coffee table before her was a cylindrical cake thickly iced. Some words had been piped on to the faintly concave surface. Upside down, Goldsmith read *Happy Birthday* and remembered.

"How do you do, Mr. Goldsmith," said Mrs. Housman, completely self-possessed. "I'm pleased you could come after all."

"Happy Birthday," said Goldsmith awkwardly. Dora was looking at him expectantly.

"I made the cake and bought Mummy a bottle of scent," she said. "She didn't get much else, but Uncle Rodney bought her that bracelet."

Goldsmith looked at the thick corrugated gold band whose expensive weight seemed to be pinning the fragile wrist to the arm of the chair.

"Your brother?" he said. Or Housman's—the only child?

"No. Just an honorary uncle," said Mrs. Housman. Suddenly Goldsmith felt a pang of something he distantly identified as jealousy. He realized Dora was still watching him expectantly. The reason why was now clear.

"I couldn't think of any present to buy, I'm afraid," he said. A shadow of disappointment passed over the girl's face.

"So I thought perhaps, instead, some kind of treat," he went on, extemporizing awkwardly. "For both of you, I mean."

It seemed important to include the girl. Her mother smiled politely but Dora was very excited.

"You mean, go out somewhere? Oh, where? On my last birthday, Daddy took me to the Tower of London in the train."

"You're very kind, Mr. Goldsmith," said her mother. "Did you have somewhere special in mind?"

"Well, if the Tower's out," said Goldsmith, emboldened, "I thought the cinema perhaps. Or a meal. Or both. Of course if you're busy this evening . . ."

The woman thought a moment, then shook her head, smiling.

"No, I don't think so. Dora, why don't you fetch the local newspaper so that we can see what's on? Unless Mr. Goldsmith had some particular film in mind, that is."

She regarded him quizzically and he shook his head. Dora was back in a minute, the paper already open at the entertainment page.

"There's *Summer Holiday*," she announced, "and not *terribly* much else."

Goldsmith's gaze met Mrs. Housman's over the girl's head and they exchanged smiles.

"It seems," said Mrs. Housman, "that if our choice is so restricted, then we must go and see *Summer Holiday*, whatever that is."

There was an early evening performance in half an hour. Dora and her mother went to get ready and Goldsmith took the opportunity of ringing Liz. There was a ward meeting that night and he had promised to take her for a drink afterwards.

She listened in cold silence to his unconvincing explanation.

"Yes, I'll see they get your apologies," she said. "What good they'll do, I don't know. It must be pretty important, Bill, this 'private business'. It could cost you a great deal."

"I've said I'm sorry," he began again, but she cut through him.

"Forget it," she said. "I've cleared your place up a bit. Don't think you've been burgled, but I took a couple of your suits to the cleaners. And I got the GPO to fix your phone."

"Thanks," he said. "That was quick!"

"Yes. I told them it was essential to your vital council business. I managed to sound quite convincing. See you, Bill."

She rang off abruptly. With a sigh, Goldsmith replaced the phone and returned to the lounge to wait for his guests.

He did not enjoy the cinema much. While he could see the two females, observe Dora's pleasure and her unsuccessful attempts to contain it, and her mother's much less revealed pleasure in that pleasure, all was well. But in the darkness of the cinema thoughts and images arose to blur the cheerful pictures flickering on the screen.

At Mrs. Housman's prompting, he bought fish and chips after the cinema performance and they ate them in the Land-Rover on the way home.

Back in Greenmansion they drank cocoa and listened to Dora talking about school. She was at a private school at the moment but now at the age of secondary transfer a decision had to be made. Housman, it seemed, had planned a continuation of private education for her. His widow was not so clear in her mind. Goldsmith offered the official party line, aware as he always was of the difference between official policy and practice at all levels. She listened politely but he felt he had made no impression on her.

Dora had yawned several times but her mother made no attempt to send her to bed and she herself probably felt it too undignified to volunteer in the presence of a visitor. Finally recognizing that Dora would remain downstairs as long as he stayed, and uncertain whether to be flattered or offended by this, Goldsmith joined in one of the girl's yawns with deliberate parody and rose to go.

"It's been a lovely birthday," said Dora. "For Mummy, I mean."

"It has indeed," said Mrs. Housman. "All the nicer for being such a surprise. Thank you, Mr. Goldsmith."

She showed him to the Land-Rover. As they stood together in the chilly autumn darkness, Goldsmith said, "By the way, when I was here on Saturday, there was a chap leaving; Munro, I think it was. I'm sure we've met and I've been trying to place him ever since."

He paused, interrogatively.

"I hope you didn't come all this way just to check a memory," she said with a laugh.

"Of course not," he said, rather over-sharply. "It just came back to me as we came out of the door."

He climbed into the Land-Rover. She held the door open.

"You may well have met him. It depends what you've been up to, Mr. Goldsmith."

"What do you mean?"

"Munro is an enquiry agent, a private detective you might say. I employed him to look into a small matter on my behalf. Does that fit with your memory of him?"

"Yes, yes. In a way I think it does."

She shut the door and stepped back. He raised his hand in acknowledgment and moved slowly down the drive. His last remark had not been a lie. He recalled now where he had first seen the man.

They had bumped into each other outside the Kirriemuir Hotel on the night of Housman's death.

It all fitted, he thought as he drove home. She had suspected her husband was fishing in other ponds and hired Munro to check on him. He must have just seen Housman safely to his room that night and been on his way to whatever seedy boarding-house private detectives slept in when they bumped into each other. And presumably their second encounter at Greenmansion had stirred some responsive chord in his mind also.

But it did not explain why he had decided to break into the cottage. If the coincidence had appeared suspicious to him, the simple thing to do was tell the police. Perhaps, thought Goldsmith, he had some naïve *Boy's Own* idea of showing how clever he was by presenting the police with a neatly solved murder. But his own brief acquaintance with the man did not suggest he was a *Boy's Own* type.

The puzzle was still unsolved when he got back to the cottage. The place was transformed. He realized he had not noticed how untidy it must have become, and he felt that mingled pang of guilt and irritation the unasked-for but necessary services of others always gave him. Even his clothes must have been neglected for longer than he recalled. Liz had neatly stacked the rubbish from his suit pockets on the dressing-tale top and it formed a sizeable pile.

He thought of ringing to thank her. She deserved better treatment than he'd been giving her lately, he told himself, but he recognized that the state of incipient sexual excitement he found himself in had a lot to do with it also. He glanced at his watch. Only 9.45. Time for a drink on neutral territory, then they could see which way the wind was blowing.

She answered the phone rather irritably, saying she had just got in after a hard night. He found himself persuading her to meet him and when she finally capitulated he was angry rather than triumphant. His head had begun to ache again and the sexy feeling had evaporated completely, but it was impossible not to go.

The noisy, smoky atmosphere of the crowded bar convinced him still further it had been a bad move. There was no sign of Liz, but for the second time in two days he came face to face with Cyril Fell. This time the man was full of beer and made no attempt at evasion.

"Councillor," he said. "*Councillor* Goldsmith, Protector of the Weak."

"I've told you before," said Goldsmith irritably. "Not here. I asked you to my cottage for a chat the other Sunday but you didn't come."

"Changed my mind," said Fell. "Had a chat with someone else. Made me think. I can put two and two together."

He nodded sagely and glowered accusingly at the same time.

"What the hell are you talking about?"

"Don't swear at me, *Councillor*. Your little game's just about up. They're on to you, I reckon. You and all these other sods. I never thought your finger'd be in the pie too, but there's no telling."

"I don't understand a word you're saying," said Goldmsith helplessly. But Fell pushed by him and disappeared through the door, passing Liz on her way in.

"What's up?" she asked. "Fell still wanting you to be the people's champion?"

"I don't think so," he said. "He seems to be trying me for quite another role at the moment."

He laughed, but he felt far from humour. He felt alone and menaced and Liz's company was suddenly very desirable. Something of this must have sounded in his voice when he suggested that she should come home with him, for she looked at him strangely before answering.

"All right," she said. "But you asked me, remember."

"I'll remember," he said.

# CHAPTER XIV

THEY PASSED the night in a violence of passion which surprised Goldsmith and might, he thought wryly, even have satisfied Templewood. The bedclothes were a disaster area in the morning, but Liz's impulse to order his life was so strong that when he returned from the bathroom he found her, still naked, making the bed with hospital expertise. On an impulse more iconoclastic than erotic, he pushed her forward on to the smooth counterpane, but she rolled aside and away from him and resumed her work.

"No time," she said. "Now for God's sake, Bill, try to *keep* this place tidy. It's not difficult, just a little effort every day."

She began pulling on her clothes with more speed than care. Her complete lack of the usual feminine narcissism had once seemed attractive, but now he found himself saying bitingly, "Tidiness should begin at home."

She missed the point and nodded.

"That's right. Look at that junk there. All out of your pockets. Now, are you just going to let it lie there till the suit comes back from the cleaners and then put it in the pockets again?"

"Probably."

But he was beginning to feel that angry-guilty feeling again and he sat down to sort out the rubbish hoping to salve both irritations. After a while the task assumed a certain archæological interest and he made a separate pile of "finds". The most ancient positive identification was of a ticket for the Labour Club's

Christmas Draw in 1956, but he suspected that a scrap of flaking card might be the remains of a genuine Festival of Britain Exhibition ticket.

"This lot rubbish? Right," said Liz, and swept his past into a paper bag.

"Oh, dump the lot," he said irritably.

"What about this?" she asked, and handed him a blue envelope folded in half.

There was a name on it. He stared in disbelief then looked assessingly at Liz to see if she had any idea what she had done. But she had turned away with her spoils safely trapped in the bag.

Written on the envelope was *Mr. N. Housman.*

Now he remembered taking the letter out of Housman's briefcase, hesitating about reading it, being diverted by the discovery of Housman's passport, and finally having the thing put completely out of his mind by the appearance of Housman himself.

He heard Liz descending the stairs and quickly he opened the envelope. It was dated "Saturday" and written on Kirriemuir Hotel paper.

*Dear Mr. Housman,* he read. *I'm sorry you were unable to wait in for me this morning. I shall try again after dinner tonight, but regretfully that will be our last chance of meeting as I must travel north first thing in the morning. I trust you have combined business and pleasure today as profitably as you did yesterday.*
                                    *Yours etc.,*


                                    *P. K. Munro*

He read it through twice, then lay back on the bed to consider its implications. It took him only a few minutes to come up with a theory. Methodically he checked through it, testing its viability.

Munro is hired by Mrs. Housman to check up on here erring husband. He amasses evidence of Housman's misdeeds, but does not pass it on. Instead he takes the opportunity of Housman's visit to London to contact the object of his investigation and invite a

deal. Probably the initial contact was by phone. In
fact, thought Goldsmith, conjuring up the details of
his Friday night vigil at the hotel, he may have seen
Housman take the call.

But Housman is a cool customer, not to be pan-
icked. On Saturday he goes his own way, ignoring
Munro's request that they should meet. Munro does
not give up so easily, but, calling at the hotel and
finding that Housman is out, he scribbles this note, its
phrasing expertly innocuous, but containing threats
that must have been clearly apparent to its receiver.

So Munro calls that evening. The interview must
have gone badly to judge by his angry appearance
outside the hotel. It also explained a certain cryptic
quality about Housman's reaction to his presence,
thought Goldsmith. *How many of you are there?* he
had asked in mock incredulity: No, he was not a man
who would panic easily.

Nor was Munro, but he must have felt considerable
unease when he heard of Housman's death. If the
police came across the letter in Housman's belongings,
their interest in him could have been embarrassingly
keen. But nothing happens. He must have been very
relieved, and just as puzzled. Doubtless when he visited Greenmansion to give his final (negative?) report,
he had created some chance to take a look at Housman's belongings, sent up from London. Among them
he would find no letter.

Then came the chance meeting with Goldsmith and
he must have begun to wonder. He had left Housman
alive, possibly derisively amused by his attempted blackmail. On the hotel steps he meets someone he now
discovers to be connected with his client's husband.
And minutes later, the husband is dead.

Curiosity, as well as possible self-interest, must have
induced him to search the cottage. But at least it was
understandable and a lot better than having one of
Vickers's men crawling around the place.

"For Christ's sake!" said Liz from the door. "What's
the point of my making the bed if you're going to
wallow all over it before you go to work?"

"Sorry," he said. "Is that the time? I must rush. I'll see you tonight."

He pecked Liz on the cheek, seized the cup of coffee she had brought upstairs with her and drank it as he finished his dressing on the stairs. Liz, far from being offended by his casual manner, seemed to sense something uxorial in it and contented herself with shouting after him without heat, "I've got a job, you know!"

He was far from sure what to do about Munro. There were dangers in every course, but to do nothing might be most dangerous of all. Halfway through the morning he called Directory Enquiries and got Jennifer Housman's number. An hour later he decided that more rehearsal was just going to make him sound as unconvincing as a washing-powder commercial, and dialled.

Mrs. Housman answered, her cool, high voice immediately recognizable. She sounded pleased to hear from him, and unsurprised. Nothing appeared to surprise her. He felt an impulse to try her with *I think your husband may have been a Major in Hitler's SS*. She would probably still have remained unsurprised and that would have given him even more cause for worrying speculation, the nature of which had already changed from its relatively simple origins.

They chatted a while. Dora had talked about the unexpected "treat" all through breakfast and expressed a hope that Goldsmith would soon come back and do a hand-print for her.

"I'm flattered," said Goldsmith.

"She needs a masculine presence somewhere in the offing," said Mrs. Housman evenly.

"By the way," said Goldsmith, "we may be needing to hire an investigator at the office. A small matter, but I wondered about that fellow Munro. Do you know anything about his background? Was he ever a member of the police force, for instance? I believe a lot of them were."

"Yes, I think he was," she answered. "I believe he used that as a selling line when I first contacted him."

"You don't sound very impressed."

There was a short pause before she answered, "No, I can't say I was."

"I see. Perhaps we should look elsewhere then. Well, back to the grind. I look forward to coming to do that handprint some time."

It was a blatant piece of invitation-fishing. But she merely brushed against the bait, gently amused, saying, "Dora will be delighted to hear that," and was gone.

So, he thought, Len the landlord had been right when he said Munro and Vickers were the same kind. Assume Munro still had contacts on the force. Would it be possible for him to find out if the break-in had been reported? And what conclusions would he draw if it hadn't been?

At lunchtime he went round to the Central Police Station and offered a bowdlerized description of the events of Sunday night. The officer who took the details seemed surprisingly unsurprised that he had let so long elapse before reporting the crime.

"Nothing missing? No. Well, someone'll come round."

"When?"

"I don't know, sir," said the man, adding poker-faced, "We'll try to take it at your speed, shall we?"

Goldsmith left, amused and also disproportionately elated. He felt that he had done something positive. It was absurd, but acting the good citizen made him feel good.

He worked hard the rest of the day and after a quick snack in the early evening, he made for the Council Chambers. There was a Finance Committee meeting at six, followed by a full Council meeting. It was a long hard session going on till after nine. Afterwards as he went into the washroom, he bumped into Jeff Malleson. There was no awkwardness, Malleson was an accomplished politician in this at least. He brushed aside Goldsmith's not very enthusiastic attempts at apology and returned with him into the washroom to discuss the meeting. The door opened behind them and Roger Edmunds came in. He was a

square-shaped ugly man in his fifties; he had twice
been Mayor and was a formidable figure in local politics; he was also Chairman of the Selection Board who
on the following Saturday would be interviewing Goldsmith and the other candidates.

"Bill," he said. "Got a moment?"

Malleson moved off, nodding approval like a pander
who had just brought a pair of coy lusters together.

"Certainly," said Goldsmith. "You want to talk
here?"

"Ay. It'll do."

Goldsmith waited expectantly. He had never liked
Edmunds much, though they had always had a fair
working relationship within the Party; and since he
had become a candidate for adoption, he had avoided
anything but the most formal and official of meetings
with the man. Edmunds was powerful, but he had not
become so by making people love him. To be known
as Edmunds's "boy" in the caucus race was a good
way to antagonize people. For instant enemies, just
add Edmunds. The thought amused Goldsmith, but he
also knew that *not* to be Edmunds's boy meant (to use
one of Templewood's images) that in the chase after
the naked blonde, you were the one carrying the anvil.

"How's things then?" said Edmunds, as though uncertain where to start. Goldsmith did not believe it.

"Grand," he said.

"Good. Bill, it's selection meeting on Saturday."

"Yes."

"We do a lot of vetting beforehand, me and the
Committee, just to make sure."

"Make sure of what?"

"That all's well. You understand? So that we know
what we need to know."

"You mean that I don't screw pigs, that sort of
thing?"

Edmunds looked offended. In his world, even gross
indecency had its own rules and conventions.

"If you like. And we listen. You get a lot of gossip
in a place like this, but people listen to it, so we've got
to as well. Do you know a man called Vickers?"

The question was such a shock that Goldsmith heard himself draw in his breath.

"Yes," he said. "Inspector Vickers, you mean?"

"That's it. So you've met him?"

"I have. Two or three times."

"What did you talk about?"

Time for a bit of indignation, thought Goldsmith. Here in Yorkshire the rules of social intercourse permitted blunt direct questioning, but they also permitted blunt direct answers.

"That's my bloody business. What do you want to know for?"

"That's been talk," said Edmunds. "Look, lad, it's for your own good I'm asking, for everybody's good. Believe me."

He sounded and looked genuinely concerned and Goldsmith was touched in spite of himself.

"What kind of talk?" he asked.

"About the way contracts have been given out by this Council," answered Edmunds.

"Oh that! You mean Cyril Fell's still stirring things!"

"You know about it then?"

"Know? What is there to know? I know that Fell . . . hold on, last time we met he said . . . is that it? Because Vickers talked to me a couple of times, people think I'm being investigated on some corruption charge! How bloody half-witted can you get?"

Half-witted it might be, but it made sense. Vickers going round asking questions about him at the same time as Fell (and others?) were crying fraud; smaller things than this had started rumours to warp a man's career.

"No," he said emphatically. "It's nothing to do with that."

"Nothing? Has this man Vickers ever talked about council business with you? Or mentioned any of your fellow councillors? Or any local contractors?"

"Never. Not a word. Look, he's connected with a mutual friend who's just been widowed. If he's been checking up, it's just to make sure I'm not some layabout after her bit of money. That's all."

If your lies run parallel to the truth then geometrically (and with a bit of luck) they should never meet. Edmunds looked at him assessingly.

"You're certain?"

"Absolutely."

"Then I'm glad to hear it. You understand I had to ask, Bill. You know what it's like, people with nothing better to do, tongues clacking, I've had it myself in my time, rest assured of that!"

He clapped his arm over Goldsmith's shoulder and, still talking, led him out of the washroom. Their exit was watched by Malleson from the end of the corridor. Goldsmith recalled Mrs. Sewell's opinion of him. Perhaps there was a grain of truth in it. Certainly there was something about him now of the pander who would have preferred to stay in the room to oversee the coupling, but who still gets some kind of kick from seeing the happy pair as soon as possible after consummation.

He gave Malleson a nod and passed on with Edmunds down the corridor. The traditional post-meeting drinking session in the mayor's parlour was often a bore, but tonight the room was buzzing with more than the usual semi-official chatter. The news of Macmillan's illness and hospitalization had just been broadcast and speculation was rife. Though his mind was more concerned with what Edmunds had just said, Goldsmith poured himself a large scotch and joined in.

Liz, as usual, would have to wait.

# CHAPTER XV

TWO DAYS LATER Templewood got in touch and they arranged to meet in the White Rose once more.

Every time the bar door opened, Templewood's eyes flickered away from Goldsmith and noted who had come in. Goldsmith was used to this. His companion was the kind of man who in any public place always gave the impression of being on the look-out for more interesting and influential acquaintances than the man he was with. With a woman, on the other hand, he appeared to shut out the surrounding world and have eyes for no one else. Today, however, this watch on the door seemed to Goldsmith to derive from something more than his normal desire for re-assurance of his own importance.

They exchanged news. Templewood had been to Leeds and visited the Waterfields.

"That Agnes," he said. "Crack you like a nut if you're not careful. Still, I squeezed her pretty dry myself."

"Tempy," said Goldsmith. "I'm a big boy now. I don't need the dirty pictures any more."

Templewood laughed, unoffended.

"Sorry. Like the man said, emotion recollected in tranquillity. Where was I?"

Where he had been was one of the local newspaper offices which employed an old acquaintance who owed him a favour. Armed with the background information supplied by Agnes Waterfield, the man had agreed to do a bit of digging on Templewood's behalf.

"And this is what he got. Black market! You remember Agnes told you the police had been round to her place looking for Housman? Well, that was what it was all about. Remember what it was like after the war? You could get hold of nothing, not unless you had the contacts and the money. Then the world was your oyster. I made a few killings myself!"

"Spivs," said Goldsmith.

"What?"

"I can see you in the loud jacket with the padded shoulders, Tempy."

"You're very cocky today, young Billy," said Templewood coldly.

Yes, I am, Goldsmith found himself agreeing internally to his surprise. It was as if deep down he had made a decision of some importance, but it had not quite reached his consciousness yet.

Templewood continued, sticking now to facts only. Housman had been suspected of being involved with a large well-organized black market set. The police had got fairly close to him, but never near enough for an arrest. And by the time they decided he'd be worth questioning, he'd moved on.

"I reckon he knew the cops were sniffing around and there's a faint hint that he had some kind of disagreement with his partners. The police weren't the only people who came looking for him, Agnes says. No, I reckon he had a policy disagreement and took off with a bit more than his share. He seems to have been a bright boy and he could see that, once rationing disappeared and things got better in the early 'fifties, the time had come to specialize. So off he went to the building trade."

"A wise choice," said Goldsmith. "With the Tories back in and ready to start one of their pseudo booms as soon as possible, there were fortunes to be made, especially to a guy with the right contacts."

Templewood raised his bushy eyebrows appreciatively.

"I was forgetting you're a politician, Billy boy. All going well there?"

"Yes."

"Good. So where are we? Housman seems to have the right credentials for old Nikolaus, doesn't he?"

"Does he? So do a million others then. Including you."

"Let's do without the holier-than-thou bit, Billy," said Templewood, drawing patterns in spilt beer with the stumpy end of his short middle finger. "One more thing. Agnes thinks he went to the Continent in 1949 or 50. Every little helps, eh, as the actress said to the choir boy. Well, your turn. What have you been up to then? Self-help's best, they say and it's you we're trying to protect, isn't it?"

The ironic rebuke stung Goldsmith in spite of himself.

"I've been having my little adventures too."

Briefly he described the events of Sunday night and his discovery of Munro's identity. Templewood listened in disapproving silence till he finished.

"This is what comes of you going to Housman's house," he said mildly. "That's where he saw you."

"I had to go in that day," said Goldsmith defensively. "It would have looked suspicious otherwise. You agreed."

"But you've been back since, you say. And talked on the telephone. That's not what you'd call discreet, is it? For Christ's sake, you don't know what you might be stirring up!"

"What do you suggest then, Tempy?" he asked.

"Step back from it for a bit, that's all. Don't do anything for a while till things settle and we can see a bit of daylight. Look, the important thing for you is still, was Housman Hebbel? Right?"

Goldsmith didn't answer immediately and Templewood repeated impatiently, "Right?"

"I suppose so."

"Suppose? What's that mean?"

"There are other things."

"What's getting into you, Billy? It's simple. Either it was Hebbel, in which case it was a happy accident; or it wasn't, in which case it was an unfortuante accident.

Now it would be nice to know. OK. I see that. And we'll keep nibbling away at it till something gives. But we've got to keep it cool, there's no point in pulling the plug on ourselves. So from now on, keep away from that house, don't even telephone; forget this Munro character, he won't bother you, not while he suspects you've got that letter. Just concentrate on nationalizing brothels or something for a while. OK?"

He raised his glass as for a toast and looked expectantly at his companion. Goldsmith turned his tankard slowly round in front of him, watching the changing pattern on the suddy surface of his beer.

"I don't think I can do that," he said.

Templewood lowered his glass.

"What?"

"I don't think I can let go so easily."

"Why the hell not? Look, I'm in this as well. Is there anything you haven't told me?"

Goldsmith chose his words carefully.

"I feel some kind of obligation to Mrs. Housman and her daughter."

Slowly Templewood relaxed and his lips began to curve into a smile.

"Well, well! So that's it! Why didn't you say, Billy boy? So you're after a bit of the old monkey-on-the-stick!"

"I didn't say that," said Goldsmith.

"No, of course you didn't. You've got this funny old-fashioned moral thing, haven't you, Billy? It's not tip-and-run for you. You're an endless-Test man if ever I saw one. OK, Billy, don't get annoyed. You're talking to an old campaigner, I've got the scars. So you fancy the widow. Well, why not? But it'll wait. Don't you see that? I mean, Christ, she's only been widowed a couple of weeks. Even in these fast times, you can hardly start making advances already. And it's not going to help your suit if she finds out you killed hubby, is it?"

Goldsmith finished his drink.

"I suppose I ought to assure you that if anything

goes wrong, I'd keep you out of it, Tempy. But sometimes I remember more strongly than others that it
was you that got me into it in the first place. So
perhaps you've got cause to be worried."

He rose to go, but Templewood reached out a hand
and detained him.

"I've killed no one, Billy. If I had to lie low for a
bit, I'd be as happy in Cannes or Acapulco as I am
here, but they're not very good places for conducting
an election campaign from, so I'm told. Think on."

"I've not been adopted yet," said Goldsmith indif-
ferently.

"And if you are? You don't fool me, Billy boy. It's
what you want, what you've always wanted."

"Perhaps so," said Goldsmith. "Let's keep in touch."

He disengaged Templewood's hand and made for
the door. As he shouldered it open, he glanced back.
Templewood had risen and was leaning on the bar
talking confidentially to the middle-aged barmaid who
in Goldsmith's eyes always seemed to have been selected to match the shiny tiled discomfort of the place.
Now she was simpering with mock coyness at something Templewood had said.

You had to give it to him, thought Goldsmith. He
knew his women.

But he might be wrong about his men.

For the first time in three nights, Goldsmith got through
his business before nine o'clock, or rather he abandoned it then. The news of Macmillan's resignation
that afternoon had provoked so many people to contact him that he began to wonder if he were on the
Tory short-list for Premier. Liz did not call. He had
seen little of her since Monday and he slowed down
guiltily as he passed her house but the place was in
darkness. Relieved, he drove on.

Something had to be done about that situation, but
he was far from sure what it was. Perhaps Mrs. Sewell
was right and marriage was the answer. Marriage gave
a woman status whatever happened, whereas to go on

as they were, with love (at least, *his* love) dying and
only fornication constant, turned Liz into his whore.
Not that he had any objections to whores; a whore
might become your friend, but that little parcel of
prejudices, codes and reactions which some hasty an-
gel had dropped into his cradle did not permit him to
accept the reverse.

He thought now of Sandra Phillips, Housman's
whore. It was a fascinating word. He couldn't shake it
out of his mind. It was fairly clear now that she hadn't
talked. Someone would have been taking a very close
look at all of Housman's acquaintances if she had, or
rather, an even closer look than Vickers appeared to
be doing.

He wondered if Jennifer Housman knew about Sandra. Perhaps Munro had after all fulfilled his contract
and provided her with a file containing full details of
her husband's perversions. Was it possible to be married to a man for ten years and not to know that he
liked being beaten? If he were Hebbel, then almost
certainly he liked to beat too.

Suddenly Goldsmith found himself hoping that she
did know, that Munro had given her the whole file and
that she had been revolted. If Housman were an unhappy memory for her also, then what did his own
knowledge matter? One thing was certain. He was
through with all this half-witted amateur detection. He
had been floundering out of his element for too long
and it was time that he let the experts resolve the
matter.

When he got back to the cottage, he went straight
upstairs and took Munro's letter from its hiding-place.
Handling it as little as possible, he snipped off the
letter-heading, Housman's name and Munro's signa-
ture, then slid it carefully into a fresh envelope.

Downstairs, he sat at his bureau and after some
thought penned a letter.

*Dear Colonel Maxwell,*
  *I am sorry to trouble you with what is almost cer-*

*tainly a figment of my imagination, but shortly after the
reunion I met a man who seemed to me strongly to
resemble Nikolaus Hebbel. It's absurd, I know, and
probably it was helped by you talking about Hebbel
that night, but I haven't been able to get this resemblance out of my mind. I have got hold of a letter
which the man has handled and I wondered if you
could possibly check the fingerprints on it against
Hebbel's (I remember you saying that his were on
record). This is a time-wasting imposition, I realize,
but it could prevent my worry from becoming an
obsession!*

He ended with a few platitudes, signed the letter, put
it and Munro's note in another envelope and addressed
it to Maxwell at the War Office.

He felt a great sense of relief as he did so. Perhaps
this was the decision he had sensed earlier his sub-
conscious had arrived at. His efforts at detection had
perhaps been vitiated by his basic reluctance to find
out the truth. But now that he could believe Housman
*qua* Housman had been a shoddy piece of work, either
way the truth could not hurt.

I am adaptable enough to be a good politician, he
thought suddenly. But the moment of self-analysis was
interrupted by someone at the door.

Liz, he thought in annoyance.

He went to the door and opened it.

"Good evening, sir," said Inspector Vickers, "I believe you had a burglary."

"Do they always send people of your rank?" wondered Goldsmith as they sat down in the living-room.
Vickers had inspected the kitchen window, peered
into the garden, asked a few questions about the lay-
out of the house and the surrounding countryside,
and gratefully accepted the offer of a scotch.

Goldsmith knew the answer to his question already,
but felt, for the time being anyway, he had better play
Vickers's game and hope the rules would emerge.

"Not always, no," said the Inspector. "But when I heard about your spot of bother, I thought, two birds with one stone."

He stretched his long legs luxuriatingly before him, forcing Goldsmith to retreat slightly, and sipped his drink.

"Now, nothing was taken, you say?"

"Nothing I've noticed."

"Not *yet*," said Vickers.

"What do you mean?"

"Well, it's always possible that later you will notice something's missing."

He said this with a half-smile on his face, as if inviting complicity, but Goldsmith without difficulty held his look of blank incomprehension till Vickers was constrained to elaborate.

"Something small. Or papers perhaps. Something you don't know you've lost until you have to look for it."

"I suppose you know about these things," said Goldsmith.

"Yes. So, your man smashed a window to get in?"

"Well, you saw the kitchen."

"I saw a window that had a bit of cardboard stuck in it, yes. An unlucky window that. I seem to recall it was broken on my first visit here."

So he had noticed, thought Goldsmith. Bloody Hawkeye.

"Yes," he said. "The burglar just had to push the cardboard in. I hadn't replaced the glass."

"Fortunate, that. For him I mean. How did it get broken in the first place? Not another burglar?"

He laughed pleasantly as he spoke, but Goldsmith was angry. He was discovering that when you only let a little bit of the truth show, it hurts disproportionately deeply to have that fragment questioned.

"No. Just an accident. Look, Inspector, I've got a bit of a complaint to make."

"Really? Against whom?"

"Against you," said Goldsmith emphatically. He

didn't mind cat-and-mouse, but you had to take turn about.

"You came round to see me in the first place because you'd met me at Mrs. Housman's and were interested in checking on a stranger who turned up out of the blue, claiming acquaintance with her husband. Right?"

"Carry on, sir. It's your house. And your excellent whisky."

Vickers helped himself to more.

"So you make enquiries. I don't blame you, that's your job and in this case it was aimed at protecting the interests of a young woman just widowed. Now, I trust your enquiries have shown I'm a fairly respectable citizen."

"More. *Very* respectable; and responsible too."

"I'm flattered. But you've been less than discreet, Inspector. I'm in public life, and at this particular moment I'm even more exposed to scrutiny than public figures normally are."

"Because of the Selection Board?"

"I thought you'd know. Well, it's no secret. Nor are your enquiries, and they've bothered people, important people. Up here it's generally reckoned that there's no smoke without fire, and naturally in my case they look for the fire in the Town Hall."

"Naturally," agreed Vickers.

"So I'd be grateful if you'd stop asking questions about me, or better still go out of your way to make it clear to one or two people that in your eyes I am *still* a respectable, and responsible, citizen."

"I see," said Vickers. "Well, well. Naturally I'm sorry if people have misunderstood the drift of my enquiries. By the way, Mr. Goldsmith, what were you doing in London the weekend of Housman's death?"

This was unexpected. Goldsmith's glass was at his lips which gave him a measure of concealment that he badly needed.

"Was I?" he asked, steadily. "Yes. I suppose I was. It must have been the weekend of my regimental reunion."

"Let me see," said Vickers, staring at the ceiling as though flicking over the pages of some mental note-book, "that would be the Saturday. But you went down a little earlier, I believe. The Thursday, wasn't it? Why was that, sir?"

"No particular reason. I had a bit of time coming. Thought I'd do some shopping, see a show. The provincial's dream of Town."

Vickers smiled. It was an interested, homely, benevolent smile fit to grace the face of matriarchal royalty examining the wares on a Mothers' Union Bring-and-Buy stall.

"See anything good?" he asked.

"No," said Goldsmith. "The things I was interested in were booked up."

"It's always the way. You didn't happen to run into Mr. Housman at all while you were down there, did you?"

"No, I didn't. Why should I?"

It was too acerbic and merited Vickers's flicker of surprise.

"Why not? It was usually in London that you met Mr. Housman, that's what you told his widow, I believe?"

"Yes. I had met him there. But not this time."

"You're sure?"

"Of course I'm sure." He was deliberately emphatic. If Vickers had some information, he wanted to force it out. But the Inspector merely nodded.

"Good. Well, I must be going. Thanks for the whisky. We'll keep in touch about your break-in."

He rose and placed his glass on the bureau, looking down at the envelope addressed to Colonel Maxwell. Goldsmith felt an impulse to ask him to post it, but suppressed it easily. You could be too clever.

"What's the latest on poor Housman?" he asked instead. It seemed a reasonable question from an old acquaintance.

"You hadn't heard? The inquest was re-opened to-day. No new evidence was offered. Nothing to indicate suicide, so they said 'accidental death'."

"Accidental death," echoed Goldsmith, trying to keep the relief out of his voice.

"Yes. He'd had a few drinks in the bar, it seems. Not much, but it'd help. He probably either stumbled against the curtains or was even sitting on the sill and just lost his balance. Dangerous these low windows."

Goldsmith's mind was moving at the double. Was Vickers still playing some subtle game or was he as happy as he appeared to be with the verdict? And if the latter, then what had he in fact been doing since Housman's death? His altruistic concern to protect a wealthy widow from male predators was an obvious fiction, though it had been a useful stage-prop for Goldsmith's indignation.

Suddenly it struck him how suspicious it must seem for an intelligent man to accept an obvious fiction. Vickers was making for the door.

"One thing more, Inspector," said Goldsmith casually. "I don't want to pry into official police business, but just what have you *really* been checking on in these weeks since Neil's death?"

Vickers looked at him in slight puzzlement.

"I'm surprised you ask, sir."

"Well, I have had my name taken in vain, haven't I? And you may not know how damaging in local goverment any hints of corruption can be, but . . ."

Vickers stemmed the indignant flow.

"Excuse me, sir, I meant I'm surprised you *needed* to ask, especially since these rumours got back to you."

"What do you mean?" asked Goldsmith, frightened now.

"Among Mr. Housman's papers in his hotel room, we found certain letters and documents pertaining to J. T. Hardy's, Mr. Housman's development company. By chance the investigating officer in London was a bright young man with some legal and business training and he read between the lines a bit and that's what started us off."

"I still don't understand," said Goldsmith. "Started you off doing what?"

"Doing what you said, of course," said Vickers, with the slow, clear articulation of one who is reciting a part or talking to a dullard. "Investigating local government contracts obtained by J. T. Hardy's and any of their subsidiary companies. Looking for evidence of illegal payments, hints of corruption. From what you said I thought you must know, I thought *everyone* must know."

# CHAPTER XVI

Munro's office was on the top floor of an old block
on the east side of Sheffield in an area which, from the
evidence of decay which abounded, looked scheduled
for redevelopment. Goldsmith had driven past a couple of levelled sites, where nothing remained more
than two feet off the ground except for large boards
headed J. T. HARDY.

It was Saturday morning. At three o'clock that afternoon he was due to appear before the Selection
Board. Liz and Malleson would probably be furiously
trying to contact him but this business could not wait.

He had sat up half the night examining the implications of Vickers's parting remarks. They should have
filled him with relief. No one was concerned with the
manner of Housman's death, therefore he was in the
clear. It was an unhappy coincidence that he must
have appeared to fit so nicely into the alleged contract
fiddle that Housman had been working in South Yorkshire. But this did not bother him too much. He was
not so naïve as to believe that innocence always tri-
umphed, but he knew (and Vickers must know) that
his particular interests on the Council had never put
him in a position where he could have been of much
use to contract seekers. In any case, he got the impression that Vickers's investigations had been getting nowhere. His own appearance on the scene must have
been a little breath of oxygen to a doubtful ember, but
there wasn't much heat left now. He had thought with
smug irony how much Vickers would have given to
have been able to follow Housman round London on

the two days prior to his death. The places he had
gone, the people he had met would probably have had
a significance to the Inspector that Goldsmith could
only guess at. He had been momentarily amused.

Then he had remembered Munro.

Munro had been paid to follow Housman for weeks
beforehand. His job had been to check on his *amours,*
that was almost certain. But a trained investigator may
have noticed other things, meetings with men that after
a while became as significant to the searching eye as
meetings with women. And the note Munro had left at
the Kirriemuir may have been threatening in both
parts of its reference to combining business with
pleasure.

He saw the potential seriousness of this hypothesis
at once. To a blackmailer evidence of his victim's
sexual peccadilloes was of little use after his death.
Occasionally the family might pay for suppression, but
in this case Mrs. Housman was the person paying for
their *discovery,* presumably for use in the divorce court,
so she would hardly be likely to be worried by threats
of publication.

Evidence of corrupt business deals was a different
matter again. Goldsmith did not know enough of the
law to be sure, but he suspected that at the very least
the business reputation of J. T. Hardy's, in which Mrs.
Housman must now have a controlling interest, would
suffer greatly, thus affecting her main source of in-
come. But it could be worse. Others in the company
might be involved. The profits from illicitly gained
contracts might be forfeit. The whole set-up might
collapse into bankruptcy and immediately all the Housman assets would be swept up by the Receiver.

He was not certain and he had no way of achieving
certainty. But if Munro did have evidence, then it was
probably just as powerful a threat to Jennifer Housman as it had been to her husband. More powerful, in
fact, because Jennifer was probably as uncertain about
the facts of the matter as Goldsmith was.

He had rung Greenmansion early on Friday.

"It's about the fellow, Munro, again," he had said.

"I checked carefully on him after what you said, and I've had one or two hints which have made me really worried."

"Hints of what, Mr. Goldsmith?" she had asked in her high, cool voice.

"About his honesty. Or lack of it. It struck me, well, he was working for you and if he got hold of any confidential information . . ."

"Yes?" she prompted him.

"I shouldn't like to think of him pressuring you in any way. I'm sorry. I know it's none of my business and all that . . ."

"Not at all. Your solicitude is most affecting."

She said it dead straight. It was impossible to see round her words to what she was thinking.

"I'd like to see you, if I may, to talk about it."

"Mr. Goldsmith, I like you, but I've known you only a very short time, too short I think to interest me in discussiing my private affairs with you. I'm sorry."

"OK. You're quite right, but it could be important. May I call round; please, Jennifer."

It was the first time he had used her christian name. It evoked no reaction.

"I don't see the point. I shall be busy this evening, and most of the weekend. Leave me your telephone number if you like, and should I feel in need of your advice or assistance then I can ring you. But I hardly think it likely."

It was better than nothing. He had rung her again that evening, ready to duck out of another council meeting if she had been willing to see him, but it seemed she had been telling the truth as there was no reply.

And finally he had got hold of the Trades Directory for Sheffield and looked up Munro. There was only one man of that name listed as an enquiry agent and it was to this address that Goldsmith had come on Saturday morning.

His motives were cloudy. That Munro was blackmailing Jennifer Housman, he felt certain. Her reaction had been *too* controlled. If she hadn't known what he was getting at, she would surely have evinced much more curiosity.

Her reaction to blackmail attempts was more difficult to gauge, but he felt that with Dora's as well as her own financial future at stake, she would not do anything hastily. She would at least appear to capitulate to give herself time to check the realities of the situation and look for a way out. Eventually she might turn to him for help, but it was doubtful. He was still too much of a stranger. In any case he could not wait. He didn't stay to analyse his reaction to this suspected threat to Dora and her mother, but, knight-errant-like, he had mounted his trusty Land-Rover and headed south.

As he mounted the long, shabbily-carpeted flights of stairs, he tried to work out some kind of tactics in his mind. His only real weapon was the letter, now on its way to Maxwell in London; but it was a devious weapon, as dangerous to the bearer as the victim. It was evidence that they had *both* been with Housman that night.

Perhaps in the end only some kind of physical threat would be possible and he felt ill-equipped to offer it. But he had to attempt to frighten the man off.

The carpet stopped at the top of the fourth and penultimate flight and his footsteps started echoing on bare boards. He supposed that somewhere in the world there were firms of enquiry agents who had large, glass-fronted office suites with high-class receptionists dotted among the potted palms. But a deep-rooted nostalgia for Hollywood private-eye movies or perhaps simply financial need had made Munro choose a more traditional setting.

The glass panel on the door which faced him at the top of the stairs bore the simple inscription *Munro Enquiries,* an economy of style which may have been artistic or again simply financial. The frosted glass prevented him from seeing inside, but he got an impression of stillness and silence from within.

He knocked on the glass and rattled the letter-box. There was no reply, so he turned the handle and pushed the door open. It squeaked loudly. All good private eyes, he recalled from somewhere, had doors that squeaked and/or floorboards that creaked, so that no one could come upon them unawares.

He stepped into a long, narrow room. It needed dusting, but some attempt had been made to keep it neat and tidy. A venetian blind brought a splash of plastic colour to the grey wall containing the only window, while a worn square of carpet spattered rather than splashed the floorboards with a leafy pattern which had made the sad transition from bright spring to the dank end of autumn. The furnishings offered few maintenance problems. They consisted of a table and two folding chairs which looked as if they had been stolen from a church hall. On the table was a neat pile of unopened mail.

In the good days, this had probably been a secretary/receptionist's office. Now, Goldsmith suspected, whatever time you called, the secretary was always out for lunch, or tea, or posting letters, or off, sick.

He crossed the carpet in two paces and rapped at the inner door. Again there was no answer, but the door was ajar.

He pushed it open. A faint, acrid smell tickled his nose and he sneezed.

This room was luxurious compared with the other. It contained a desk, a swivel chair, an armchair, two filing cabinets, curtains at the window and an Indian rug on the floor.

It also contained Munro whom neither creaking floorboards nor squeaking door had been able to prevent from being taken unawares. He lay face down on the floor beside the desk. Round about his right foot were the remnants of a smashed coffee cup and saucer. It looked as if he had forgotten they were on the floor by his chair, had risen, trodden on them and pitched headlong forward. His right hand, stretched out as though to break his fall, was convulsively clenched round the double element of an unprotected electric fire. That was where the smell was coming from. The fire had been on. The switch was still down, though of course the fuse in the plug would have gone. But not before a lethal voltage had been pumped through the unfortunate man.

Goldsmith circled the body carefully. Munro was dead, that was clear. The one eye that was visible was open and a trickle of blood from his nose was dry and brown. The sight of another human being dead touched him, but stronger than the no-man-is-an-island sentiment was the there-is-a-tide-in-the-affairs-of-men certainty.

Munro dead was still dangerous. Whatever he had gathered together in the way of evidence—notes, photographs, documents etc.—must be hidden somewhere. Eventually someone would find Munro and call the police. And they as professional nosers would have a good look round.

Suddenly he remembered the pile of mail on the table in the outer office.

Someone *had* come in, picked it up (perhaps it had jammed under the door), put it on the table. Not Munro. He would have brought it through here. No, someone had already found Munro and . . . what? Phoned the police? Left without doing anything? Or perhaps phoned the police anonymously from a safe distance. In which case, at any moment . . . he turned, his instinct telling him to leave.

Close by someone moved. A tell-tale floorboard creaked. Not one of those outside on the stairs, but closer.

There was another door in the room. He stepped up to it and turned the handle.

Something resisted from the other side. He pressed his shoulder to the woodwork and pushed. The pressure from inside grew. Someone was pushing back and through the open door he caught a strong whiff of perfume.

"Jennifer?" he said, stopping pushing. "It's me, Bill Goldsmith."

There was a pause. Then slowly the door opened. It led into a small cloakroom with a lavatory and wash-basin.

Standing facing him was a woman, pale-faced but contained. At first he could not put a name to her.

"Hello again, Mr. Maxwell," she said.

It was Sandra Phillips.

They postponed explanations. Each recognized in the other a strong desire not to be found here, and it was also apparent that they were both looking for something they did not want anyone else to find. Neither was successful. The filing cabinets and the desk were the only things to be searched and these were all practically empty. Unless Munro had gone to the lengths of pulling up floorboards or excavating walls to create special hiding-places, the Housman file was not here.

Goldsmith knew it was impossible to look further without leaving evidence of the search. In any case, he doubted if Munro would have taken such precautions. And time was passing quickly. Nonetheless he hesitated about leaving empty-handed, though the woman was standing impatiently by the door.

The phone rang.

They both startled visibly, then looked at each other sheepishly, their features relaxing into half-smiles.

"Time to go," said Goldsmith.

He took out his handkerchief and carefully rubbed everything he had touched.

"The police have your prints?" asked Sandra Phillips, raising her eyebrows.

"Who knows?"

The job finished to his satisfaction, he followed her into the outer office. Cautiously she opened the door and peered on to the landing.

"All right," she said.

"Wait."

He pointed to the letters on the table.

"Did you put those there?"

"Yes," she said. "I picked them up as I came in."

Quickly Goldsmith glanced through them. Bills, circulars, nothing private. He gave them a good rub with his handkerchief and after they had closed the door behind them, he pushed them through the letter-box.

"Thorough," she said. "As to the manner born."

Outside he asked if she had a car. She shook her head and he took her to the Land-Rover.

"Suppose I don't want to go with you," she asked.

"Your privilege."

He climbed into the driving seat and said nothing as she got in beside him.

Later they drank weak coffee together in the restaurant of a large departmental store, chosen because the tables were far enough apart for private conversation.

"Ladies first," he said.

"You're joking."

"All right. But you got there first."

"He was just as you saw him. It looks as if he slipped and fell against the fire. I was shocked, naturally. Then I heard you come in. I was frightened and hid."

"Naturally. What were you doing there, Miss Phillips?"

She stared at him out of her large, candid brown eyes. She was a striking woman, he thought. And smiled to himself as he recognized the accidental pun.

"Why should I tell you that?"

"So I'll tell you when it's my turn."

"Big deal. I'm a girl with a great lack of natural curiosity, Mr. Maxwell. Or is it Goldsmith? I find it helps in my business."

"Prostitution?"

"If you like."

"Of a special kind."

She looked puzzled for a moment, then laughed, showing excellent teeth. She really did project a fine, healthy, outdoor image.

"Oh yes. I'd forgotten. No, no. I'm adaptable. I give the customer what I think he needs."

It took a moment for Goldsmith to grasp what she meant.

"You mean, that morning . . ."

"I mean I knew damn well Neil Housman wasn't the kind to go around lashing out recommendations to all

and sundry. You struck me as a chancer, someone
who'd caught my name from Neil in his cups and
thought he'd try his luck."

"So you thought it'd be funny to knock hell out of
me with a cane?"

"Why not? *There's been a mistake* you said. So
polite. I was splitting myself. Then those cops came
and told me about Neil. I stopped laughing then. I
don't believe in coincidences. This is about Neil, isn't
it?"

"Yes. Ultimately. You didn't mention me to the
police then?"

"No. Why should I?"

"I might have been dangerous."

"You didn't look dangerous. But you're right. I see
that now. You might be."

"So tell me about Munro."

This time she did not demur.

Housman, it appeared, visited her regularly when
he was in London and Munro, having logged a couple
of visits and taken photographs of Housman's arrivals
and departures, had decided that more evidence would
be useful. He had somehow got into the flat and
bugged the main rooms. Naturally he had recorded
not only Housman's visits, but the visits of one or two
other men also, and had had the curiosity and the
industry to find out who they were.

"Who were they?" asked Goldsmith.

She looked at him coldly.

"I'm selective and I'm expensive," she said. "My
visitors get from me what they want. They also get
confidentiality."

Ten days earlier she had received some pieces of
tape through the post. She had played them and recognized instantly how dangerous they were. A telephone call had followed. She had answered cautiously,
wanting to find out all she could about this man. It
appeared that Munro had recognized that tapes themselves were far from perfect blackmail levers, even
when supported by documentation. The real impact
would come from photographs, and encouraged by

Sandra Phillips's response on the phone, he had gradually during the course of three or four calls approached the point of inviting her partnership.

"I think his first thought was to put the bite on me, you know, take a pimp's cut without doing any of the work. Me, all I wanted to do was keep him off my customers."

"Very noble," said Goldsmith.

"Us whores don't understand irony," she said. "At my level, reliability in every sense is important. It wouldn't matter that it wasn't my fault; the slightest sniff of trouble and I'd be out of business, with a choice between retiring to Eastbourne on my savings or joining the short-time girls round the clubs. So, I led him on and finally arranged a meeting with him up here. I booked in at my hotel last night and found a note waiting for me, just a time and an address. Munro's office it turned out to be. I got there early. I hoped there might be a chance to look around, but I wasn't really bothered. Once I'd got him spotted, I've plenty of friends who would be happy to do me a favour."

"Perhaps one of them did," suggested Goldsmith.

"No," she said, shaking her head. "No one knew. And all I wanted were those tapes and anything else he had. No violence. Anyway, it was an accident."

"So it would appear."

He finished his coffee and glanced at his watch.

"I must be going," he said.

"Hold on! It's your turn. You weren't there just to read the meter either!"

"No." He looked at her speculatively. "Look, it's simple. Munro was trying to blackmail a friend of mine. I went round to sort things out. OK?"

"Mister, compared with that, you've had the story of my life!"

"How long are you staying in Sheffield?" he asked.

"How long would you stay if you didn't have to?"

"All right." He grinned at her. "Give me your London number. I think I may be able to sort all this out with no further bother, *and* get your tapes back.

Just sit tight and go on as before till you hear from me. A couple of days, that's all."

She lit a cigarette and stared at him through the smoke.

"What do you know that I don't?" she asked.

"Confidentiality is a virtue in all kinds of business," he replied. "Remember, do nothing."

He looked back as he paid for their coffee at the cash-desk on the way out. She had put the cigarette out already. It had been some kind of stage-prop. He raised his hand as he left, but she did not reply.

When he reached his Land-Rover, he realized that he had made no attempt to discover what, if anything, she really did know about Housman's origins. For the moment, it just did not seem important.

# CHAPTER XVII

FINDING MUNRO DEAD had been a shock for more than one reason. Like Sandra Phillips, he didn't believe in coincidence. He had not been lying to her when he said that he hoped to get hold of her tapes. Almost certainly these would be with the Housman stuff and that was what he wanted to get his hands on. But before he put himself at risk by discovering where Munro's private residence was and attempting a search there, he was first going to make sure that the journey was really necessary.

He was heading for Greenmansion.

This morning the house looked sad, like a beached ship. The recent bad weather had torn many of the leaves from the trees and they patterned the lawn with drifts and curls like the seaweed and flotsam left by a retreating tide. He recalled that Jennifer had claimed she would be busy most of the weekend and when he rang the bell, its distant tinkle seemed swallowed instantly by emptiness. He didn't bother to ring again but was turning away when the door opened.

"Hello," said Dora.

"Hello," he said.

She looked at him very seriously.

"I was practising the piano," she said.

"I'm sorry if I've disturbed you. I didn't hear you playing."

"I wasn't actually pressing the notes down," she explained. "It gives you greater delicacy of touch."

She produced the phrase as though the words were inseparable.

"I suppose it must. But how do you know you're playing the right notes?"

"You hear them inside your head."

"Is your mother in?" was the best reply he could produce.

"No. Uncle Rodney called and took her out."

"Did he now? And they've left you alone?"

"Not really. My friend Anabelle is ten today and her father is taking a party of us swimming and then we're going to have lunch. They're going to pick me up on the way. Mummy told me not to open the door to anyone else, but I saw it was you."

"Well, thank you. May I come in?"

She stood aside and he stepped into the hall. He disliked taking advantage of the girl's being alone in the house, but ultimately it would save everyone a great deal of embarrassment if a quick look around revealed that Munro's Housman file had been retrieved. What it would tell him about Jennifer, he did not care to contemplate, but at least it would avoid the certainties of confrontation.

"How old is Uncle Rodney?" he asked, partly to make conversation and partly to try to still twinges of jealousy he felt once again.

"Oh, let me see. Much older than you."

It was said in a manner which put his own age at some unimaginable extreme of antiquity, but it was a comfort for all that.

"How soon will your friend be here?"

"She's late already. She's very bad at time. Would you like to do a hand-print while you're here?"

"That would be nice."

She led him upstairs, talking all the while with a self-possessed courtesy obviously imitative of her mother, but with enough of herself in it to avoid mere parody.

When they reached the door on the first-floor landing which led to the attic stairs, Goldsmith paused.

"I'll just pop into the bathroom," he said. "You go on and get the paint ready."

"All right," she agreed.

He waited till he heard her reach the top of the stairs then moved along the landing, pushing open doors till he found the master bedroom. If the file were hidden anywhere, this seemed the most likely spot. Houseman probably had a safe somewhere in the house, but his own (admittedly limited) experience of women led him to believe that when it came to hiding things, they would rely on their own ingenuity rather than masculine strongholds.

He went quickly round the room. The animal-pelt coverlet was still in use. That apart, the room's atmosphere was almost wholly feminine and he wondered whether this had evolved since, or predated, Housman's death. The dressing-table, wardrobe and tallboy produced nothing. He felt like a nasty old man as he ran his fingers through the neatly folded underclothes in the scented drawers, but he had to admit to a certain gentle stimulus.

He was down on his knees looking under the mattress when Dora came into the room.

"Couldn't you find the bathroom?" she asked.

"Yes. I'm sorry," he said, standing up quickly and feeling an unfamiliar flush surging up his cheeks. "This door was open and I saw a beetle."

It was a feeble story but Dora took it in her stride.

"Did you catch it?" she asked.

"No. I'm afraid it got away."

"Under the mattress?"

"I don't know. I just thought I'd look."

"I suppose it could be among the bedclothes," she said calmly. "Are you ready for your hand-print yet?"

Meekly he let himself be ushered upstairs.

"I'm afraid I can't offer you a choice of colours," she said. "I'm trying to keep a balance and it has to be red."

She had prepared a mix of red poster-colour in a shallow dish.

"Pull back your sleeve," she said professionally. "Otherwise it might get on your jacket. Now dip your hand in and make sure you get it all over the fingers and palm. You have to kneel on the bed, but I've put a bit of newspaper down in case you drip. Are you ready?"

"I think so," said Goldsmith, lifting his hand from the dish and examining it.

Outside a horn blew. Dora went into the jungle alcove and looked out of the window.

"Bother. Here's Anabella now. I'll have to go, her father's very impatient. Can you finish by yourself? On the bottom row next to Uncle Rodney's. 'Bye."

She smiled at him and left the room. He heard her running down the stairs, and shortly afterwards the front door slammed and a car revved up, then moved off down the drive.

Goldsmith glanced at his watch. This was a piece of luck. He had a good half-hour before he needed to head back north to face the Selection Board. Time for a good poke round, but first he had better leave his hand-print.

He knelt on the bed and examined the pattern. Each print had the name of its maker written in a clear childish hand beneath it. Top left was a small delicate outline which he was sure he would have picked out as Jennifer's without the neat inscription. And next to it was a larger hand; broad palmed; strong, nervous fingers; marked *Daddy*. He thought of the letter now on its way to Maxwell and frowned. For the first time he found himself hoping positively that the man would prove *not* to be Hebbel. Whatever that might do to his own peace of mind, it would leave Dora untouched by the poison.

He shook his head and lowered his eyes, looking for old Uncle Rodney's name. There it was, right at the bottom. He pressed his hand to the wall alongside the green print Uncle Rodney had made. And as he held it there, something odd about the neighbouring print impinged itself upon his consciousness.

It was incomplete. The top knuckle of the middle finger was missing.

He was nearly thirty minutes late for the Selection Board meeting. Malleson and Liz were standing outside the Labour Club like a pair of anxious wedding guests sent out to look for a late bride.

"Where the hell have you been!" cried Liz. "I've been looking for you all morning."

Malleson was much calmer.

"It's OK. No harm done. You're third alphabetically and they've still got the first one in. Plenty of time to tidy yourself up."

Goldsmith shrugged, indifferent to either greeting, and ran his hand through his hair. Liz shrieked.

"Bill, what have you done to your hand?"

He glanced down.

"Only paint," he said. "It'll wash off."

"I hope so," said Malleson. "Keeping the red flag flying is one thing, but this lot don't actually want to see the blood of the martyred dead. Let's get in."

He put himself in their hands and ten minutes later he was judged presentable enough to join the other candidates in the waiting-room. He nodded at them and sat down next to a long-haired, sharp-faced young man whose name was Croxley, but whom he always thought of under Liz's sobriquet of "the little shit from LSE".

"Thought you'd changed your mind," said Croxley amiably.

"No. Just the traffic."

It was a lie. But then to say he'd almost changed his mind would have been far from the truth too. For a while, the Selection Board had merely been relegated to a very minor place on his scale of things-that-mattered. Indeed, it hadn't risen very far up the scale; it was just that when a man wants something to occupy his body and mind for a few hours, whatever has been timetabled comes easier than thinking of something new.

"I've been in," said Croxley. "Davis is in now. You'll be next."

He paused, clearly expecting to be asked what it was like.

"Why don't you piss off home then?" said Goldsmith.

He leaned back in his chair and closed his eyes.

At first it had been simple sexual jealousy that had flooded his body and mind as he became more and more certain that the deformed hand-print was Templewood's. He had never called, or heard any-one else call him anything but "Tempy". But he managed to conjure up an image of his name on documents and company orders. *Templewood G. R*. It fitted.

So at first it had merely seemed that Templewood, quick off the mark as ever, had exerecised his usual charm on Jennifer Housman and followed up their first meeting with a panache outside Goldsmith's capacity. But things did not quite hang together.

He had met Goldsmith coming away from Green-mansion the previous Saturday after what was allegedly his first and only visit. Yet Dora, standing in the rain at the Land-Rover window, had reminded Templewood he had promised to mend her bike. And Dora was returning *to* the house not coming away from it.

In addition he recalled the thick, expensive-looking gold bracelet which had looked so heavy on Jennifer's delicate wrist. *Uncle Rodney's present*, Dora had said. But Jennifer Housman was not the kind of woman to accept such a present from a man she had known only two days. Not even if the man were Templewood? he asked himself. He mustn't allow his own resistance to the man's charm to make him disre-gard its existence. *Any woman I can't have up against a wall in ten minutes* . . . he recalled Templewood's old boast.

But no. He could not accept this or anything like it of Jennifer Housman.

Why not? he asked himself angrily. What did he know about her?

Very little. And very little more after searching her house from top to bottom without paying much attention to concealing the traces of his search.

He had thought of sitting in the lounge, waiting till they came back, but impatience and a desire for more thinking time had sent him out of the house and brought him finally here.

*"Mr. Goldsmith."*

The tone of voice indicated that the speaker was repeating himself. He opened his eyes and looked up.

"The Board's waiting for you, Mr. Goldsmith," said Malleson from the door. He was doing the formal, neutral ushering bit.

"I'm sorry. Right."

He stood up.

"Good luck," said Croxley. "Fingers crossed."

"Why don't you piss off?" said Goldsmith again. And went through into the committee-room.

His memories of the interview were few and fragmented. There seemed to be about a dozen people on the Board, many of them familiar faces, a couple anonymous. "Straight bat," Malleson had advised in a incantatory whisper as he went through the door, but the mood was on him to swing at everything, and though some runs came, they were generally off the edge.

"What brought you into political life, Mr. Goldsmith?"

It was Edmunds who started, easing him with an obvious question.

"My mother. And a midwife. And when I first went out into our town, I wished they hadn't bothered."

A couple of laughs. Some smiles. A gaunt man, whose teeth seemed to indicate that his Socialism hadn't caught up with the National Health Service yet, drew a large question mark on the doodling sheet before him.

"Seriously, Mr. Goldsmith . . ."

"Seriously, I suppose the war."

That was the right answer, or at least the right start to the right answer. Lots of nods.

"You were captured, weren't you?"

"That's right."

There had been other tribunals, other bouts of questioning, sometimes from as many as these present, sometimes only one.

"It changed my way of thinking, I suppose. It changed a lot of people."

"So after demob, you joined the Party."

He shook his head.

"I joined the other losers."

"What?"

"I don't understand, Mr. Goldsmith." A prim lady with a WI hat. What was she doing here? "We won the election in '45."

"I won a medal in '44. I still spent eighteen months in a prison camp. No, I saw that how the world worked was by the few permanent winners letting most of the permanent losers imagine they were winning for some of the time. So I decided the thing to do was never to forget which you were. Politics reminded me."

"Do you still think you're with the losers, Mr. Goldsmith?" The speaker was a solid man in late middleage, his face darkened with a miner's small scars. Goldsmith knew something of his background. His pit had closed in the last twelve months and a new road had been put through the terrace of houses he had lived in since birth.

"Ay," he answered. "Don't you?"

So it went on. A lot of it may have got across like good social indignation, and he had neither the energy nor the inclination to attempt to communicate the turmoil in his mind now, nor at any time in the past twenty years.

"Are you happy to follow Harold Wilson?" someone asked.

He had shrugged.

"A hound'll follow a trail to a cliff's edge, but he'd be a daft dog to go over, no matter how strong the scent."

Finally, "You're not married, Mr. Goldsmith?" It was the WI hat again. Perhaps she was a spy.

"No."

"Is there any chance of a change, I mean, something definite?"

"Well, I'm not queer, if that's what you mean. As for a change, well, we live in hope."

She wouldn't let it alone.

"These questions have to be asked, Mr. Goldsmith. An MP's wife is important."

"Everybody's wife is important."

It was meant to be dismissive, but it set the heads nodding again like buttercups in a summer breeze. Even the WI's gaudy lemon flower bobbed elastically.

"How was it?" asked Malleson when he came out.

"Christ knows. Or even worse than that."

Liz took his arm and looked at him thoughtfully. She knows something's up, he thought, but felt intruded upon rather than comforted by this empathy.

He wanted to go now, but they made him wait and he did not have the will to resist.

It was nearly six when the last of the candidates got through. Then came another fifteen minutes' wait.

Finally Edmunds appeared.

"Gentlemen, we've reduced the short list to a *short* short list of three and we're going to need more time for our deliberations. The three still under consideration are Mr. Croxley, Mr. Goldsmith and Mr. Wardle. Thank you all for your courtesy and patience. Thank you."

The only name which surprised Goldsmith was his own. They really must be moronic.

"The obvious three," said Liz delighted. "I don't know why they bothered."

"Still it's cause for a third of a celebration," said

Malleson. "A couple of pints and a curry. What do you say, Bill?"

Why not? He might as well stay with the losers, he thought.

"Why not?" he said.

# CHAPTER XVIII

SUNDAY WAS a grey day. The weather was dull, he had a hangover, and even bright sunshine and good health would have been insufficient to remove the deep depression of spirit he felt.

Liz turned up at lunchtime with Mrs. Sewell close behind, examining the exterior of the cottage with a critical eye. The Land-Rover was parked at an odd angle across the front yard.

He kept them on the doorstep.

"We were going for a drink," said Liz. "How about joining us? Then lunch?"

"Not today, thanks," he said. "I'm busy. And not very hungry."

He tried to smile in reference to his unremembered excesses of the night before, but got no response.

"She's worried about you," said her mother. "Didn't like the way you looked and talked last night."

"What did I say?" he asked, suddenly alert.

"Nothing. Just reaction, I guess," said Liz. "So you won't come?"

"No, thanks. I'll see you during the week."

Liz ran a hand through her wild hair and returned to the car. Mrs. Sewell stared calmly at Goldsmith.

"She's not very sharp, our Liz, but it'll get through eventually," she said in a conversational tone.

"What will?"

"The big farewell. Only don't make it a soldier's,

172

will you? I expect you'll even manage to remain just good friends. You can go far, Billy."

She raised a hand in a semi-military salute.

" 'Bye, 'bye, bastard."

He felt wretched as he watched them drive away, but there is a limit to unhappiness beyond which its separate causes become indistinguishable, and his farewell to Liz (if that indeed was what it had been) was quickly subsumed by the general depression.

He lunched on the remnants of a bottle of scotch and afterwards followed his usual path up the ridge to the ravaged grove. Here he leaned against the middle tree and stared gloomily down at the rapid, shining river. His own thoughts drifted more turgidly and darkly. Perhaps the time had come to move. The suburban leprosy had not yet infected the village, but other things, other people, just as insidious in their own way as bricks and mortar, were pressing him hard. Perhaps the time had come for that flight to the hills which had always existed in his mind as the secret escape route to a final refuge. His purchase of the cottage had been a step in that direction, counterbalanced by his almost simultaneous political involvement. The tension had been preserved, but it could not be maintained for ever. His performance at the Selection Board the previous day must surely have eased it in one direction. His selection for the final three couldn't be anything more than a sop to local feeling. So there would be little to keep him here if he decided to go. Bow out gracefully at the next local elections, resign from his job, sell the cottage and with the proceeds and the tidy bit of savings he'd got safely invested, he could set out to find that small-holding or croft where he could prove his self-sufficiency.

Everything seemed clear. He could not understand why he had delayed so long. As if in sympathy with his mood, a wind sprang up, stirring the low cloud-cover to turbulence and moving the black branches of the dead trees into sinister life. He breathed deep, sucking in the cool air. Above him the tree creaked and groaned. He turned to go, heard a crashing splintering noise and looked up to see a six-foot length of branch tumbling down on him.

He flung himself against the bole of the tree, pressing hard against the flaking, charcoal-like bark. The branch struck his shoulder glancingly, bounced from the ground and fell against his left leg as though in a final effort to cause some damage. Neither blow was strong enough to do more than bruise, and the branch lying still on the ground looked a slight, harmless piece of firewood. But Goldsmith felt himself menaced and moved swiftly away down the hill towards the cottage.

Halfway down he stopped and looked back. His mood had switched completely and now he found himself able to laugh at his own stupidity.

Wandering around like Heathcliff, planning to become a hermit! And all because of what? A handprint! The number of men with a bit of finger missing must be enormous. Why the hell should it be Templewood's?

And even if it were, so what? Templewood was only a man, could be confronted, challenged, defeated, like any other man. It had been loose ends, which had started all this. He was not going to move on and leave any more behind. For the second time in five minutes, the future seemed completely simple.

When he got back to the cottage, he dialled the Housman number. The phone was lifted almost immediately.

"Jennifer?" he said. "Bill Goldsmith. I should like to come round to see you if I may."

"Of course," she said in her perfectly composed way. "But not today. Tomorrow evening, would that suit you?"

"Yes, fine."

"Shall we say about eight-thirty? Good. I shall look forward to that. Goodbye, Mr. Goldsmith."

The receiver was replaced.

Wearily Goldsmith climbed up the stairs to bed. It was only teatime but he felt exhausted. And he also felt as if the initiative had somehow been taken away from him once more. *Mr. Goldsmith*, she had called him, as though he were an insurance salesman making an appointment. There had been the usual absence of surprise, no reference to his visit the previous day.

He would surprise her once before they were finished. But now as he lay on his bed he felt as physically and mentally lifeless as he had done on rising from it that morning.


After a seemingly endless day at work, he returned home on Monday evening and began to prepare himself for his visit to Greenmansion. It seemed important to appear perfectly groomed, and he was shaving for the second time that day when the phone rang.

"Hello," he said.

"Goldsmith? That you? Maxwell here."

He had half expected it would be Malleson or perhaps Liz, and it took him a moment to readjust.

"Oh, Colonel. Hello."

"It was about that letter of yours. Got it on Saturday and of course I put things in train at once."

"Yes. I'm sorry to have bothered you, probably nothing I realize, but . . ."

"Not at all. You were quite right. You'd be surprised how often this kind of thing happens, and unless the chap concerned has the sense to get a proper investigation started immediately, it can often become an obsession. Consequences nasty sometimes."

There was a pause. Significant? wondered Goldsmith guiltily. But there was a crackle of paper at the other end and the Colonel's voice resumed.

"Here we are. So, when this arrived on my desk just as I was leaving this evening, I thought I'd give you a ring straightaway."

"Thank you. It's very kind . . ."

"Yes. Well, it seems there were at least three sets of

prints on that letter you sent us. Lot of them blurred of course, but three good thumb-prints. It's the way people hold a piece of paper, you see."

"Yes. Could your people idenify any of them, Colonel?" he asked urgently.

"Oh no. Sorry. I should have said. Oh no. Put your mind at rest. There's a very well-authenticated set of Hebbel's prints in existence and these bear no relationship to any of those on the letter. Well, there you are. Pity. It would have been a real turn-up for Hebbel to be found hiding in England. And for him to be spotted by one of the principal witnesses against him! Fleet Street would have loved that. Anyway, how are things with you? Well, I hope? You got home safely after the reunion? I was a bit concerned."

"Yes, thanks. I'm fine. I'm sorry to have put you to so much trouble."

"Never in the world. How are the politics, by the way? Things going well there? They're certainly very thorough when it comes to vetting their prospective candidates, aren't they?"

"What do you mean?" asked Goldsmith.

"Well, about a week ago, a police chap was round asking questions about you. War record, that kind of thing. Fellow named Villers, Vickers, something of the sort. Very interested in the reunion. Checking on your drinking habits, I shouldn't wonder! I put him right, of course. Told him you were good Prime Minister material, if that's a compliment! Still, I suppose it's comforting to know they do these things so thoroughly."

"Yes, I suppose it is," said Goldsmith.

"Good. Best of luck. See you at the next reunion if not before. Goodbye now."

"Goodbye," said Goldsmith, replacing the receiver. The earpiece was flecked with foam, reminding him that he had not finished shaving.

He had been warned, he realized. The thought made him smile. Old traditions died hard. An officer protected his men as much as possible. The thin red line could be as effective against one's own civilian authorities as against the enemy.

But the important information was that Housman was not Hebbel. It had not really penetrated yet. What did it mean to him? He was not yet able to say. There was an emptiness somewhere inside him whose dimensions were not measurable. Certainly there was no immediate in-rush of guilt and remorse. The hunt for Hebbel had at least sufficiently distanced Housman's death to put him out of range of its most devastating reactions.

It had been a game from the start. He had allowed Templewood's hysteria to infect him, then after the killing took place, it had been easier to go on playing the game than to put the pieces away and look at the realities of the situation. But now too many of the pieces had flesh and names for them to be easily swept into a box.

He finished shaving and dressed. He had collected the suits Liz had sent to the cleaners and he deliberately chose the one he had been wearing the night of the reunion. With it he wore a white shirt and his regimental tie.

He examined himself in the mirror.

At least I look a good class of insurance salesman, he thought.

He nodded at his reflection as though saying farewell. Everything he did tonight seemed to have a valedictory flavour about it. And the front door of the cottage swung shut behind him with a crash possessing the kind of finality which sends cinema audiences groping for their coats and handbags under their seats.

Greenmansion tonight was a ghost-ship, scarcely distinguishable from the dark sky which pressed close behind it. What light there was inside was smothered by thick, heavy curtains which only permitted an uncertain glow to touch the window panes. Only in one

of the dormer-windows were the curtains drawn back
and Goldsmith thought he saw a figure outlined there,
looking down on his arrival. He thought he could
work it out that it was the dungeon alcove, but it was
impossible to be sure.

Jennifer Housman greeted him at the door.

"Come in," she said. They went into the lounge. She
sat down and looked at him, making him feel as if he
were being interviewed for some household post. In
reaction he sprawled awkwardly into an armchair and
stared back at her in silence.

"I'm sorry I was not at home when you called on
Saturday," she said finally. "I got the impression from
what Dora said and from what I found on my return
that you were looking for something."

No question. No curiosity.

"I'd just been to see Munro," he said.

"You decided to employ him after all."

"Not really. He was dead."

"That must have been very distressing for you. I
don't recall seeing any report."

Nor did he. Presumably Munro had been the kind
of man who could disappear for three or four days
without being missed. Or perhaps a simple accidental
death did not rate a mention in these days of burgeon-
ing violence.

"There *was* someone alive there," he went on.

"Yes?"

"Your late husband's whore."

"Oh yes. That would be Miss Phillips?"

She smiled slightly as she said it. He felt a flicker of
anger for a moment, then it passed and he relaxed in
the chair. The way to play this was to remain equally
unperturbed.

"You knew her?"

"I know of her. You must have guessed, Mr. Goldsmith, that I hired Munro to check on my husband's
affairs with a view to divorce. His visits to Miss Phillips were mentioned in his report."

"How much did he want?"

"Munro? Oh, the normal fee. So much a day and expenses."

"No. I meant for the whole report. How much did he want to keep quiet?"

"I don't understand you."

She looked beautiful, all delicacy and strength like a seabird above a cliff edge, balancing on a column of air.

"I'm on your side, Jennifer," he said urgently. "I want to help. I know Munro had found out your husband was involved in bribing various people in local government to get contracts and that he threatened to destroy J. T. Hardy's if you didn't pay him off."

"You know more than I do, Mr. Goldsmith," she answered.

"For God's sake! Can't you see, I want to help you. Look, all I want to know is, have Munro's records been destroyed? That's why I came round on Saturday. That's what I was looking for!"

She looked at him with what to his bewilderment appeared to be real distaste.

"Is that all, Mr. Goldsmith? Just to help me? Suppose I assure you that you have nothing to worry about, that your distinguished career is in no danger. Will you have helped me enough then?"

He looked at her with incomprehension. For a moment it had seemed to him that she must know he had killed her husband. But her words could not mean that. Her words clearly meant something else, and what they meant could only be one thing. But how could they mean that. Unless . . . unless . . .

He rose to his feet and she followed suit.

"What are you trying to say, Mrs. Housman?" he demanded. "What are you implying?"

Before she could answer a new voice interrupted them.

"Well, this is cosy. Evening, Goldsmith. Nice to see you. Jennifer, I've tucked her in and told her one of my more respectable bedtime stories, but I'm sure she'd like a goodnight kiss from her mum. I'll entertain Mr. Goldsmith for a bit."

Jennifer turned, smiled at the newcomer and left the room without speaking.

"Hello, Uncle Rodney," said Goldsmith to Templewood.

# CHAPTER XIX

THEY SAT and drank whisky together like old friends newly met after long separation. And the tenor of their conversation, to start with at least, was amicable.

"You told her that I was one of the local government men involved in her husband's fiddles?"

"Not told her, exactly. Let her believe, yes. I mean, it seemed fairly obvious, Billy. Even your policeman friend thought so, didn't he? And it was a jolly good explanation of your visits here."

Templewood smiled as though inviting compliments on his cleverness.

"I see. So she doesn't know of my connection with Housman's death?"

Templewood shook his head.

"Nor of yours then?"

"Mine?" said Templewood, surprised. "I'm not connected."

"If I am, you are. Never forget that, Uncle Rodney." Templewood did not seem bothered.

"Something seems to be troubling you, Billy boy. Why don't you grab hold with both hands and show it the daylight, as the bishop said to the actress?"

"Christ, you've got a one-track mind!" said Goldsmith. "How any decent woman can look at you twice, God alone knows!"

Templewood poured himself another drink and grinned broadly.

"Is that all the trouble, Billy? Me and Jennifer? Or me and all of them? You want to know the secret! I've told you often enough, boy. Honesty! Remember the story about the shy lad who fancied this bird at a dance? His mate said, 'All right, let's try her,' walked right up to her and said, 'Fancy a jump then, girl?' She laid one on his jaw that knocked him flat. The shy lad picked him up and said, 'Christ, you must get a lot of clouts that way,' and he said, 'Ay, but I get a lot of jumps.' So you see, me, I make no secret of what I want. With you, it's all tucked away so that nobody knows. I mean, are you a success or a failure, Billy boy? Can *you* tell me?"

Goldsmith half listened, forcing himself to relax. Templewood's little speech was self-indulgence. It gave the opposition time to organize. And that they were in opposition he had no doubt now.

"I never doubted you were a good salesman, Tempy," he said.

"No? Well, I've certainly sold myself to Jennifer," said Templewood brutally.

"A bargain, I'm sure. When?"

"What?"

"When did the sale take place? How long have you known her?

Templewood looked at him cautiously.

"You know me, Billy boy. Greased lightning. Remember the ten-minute rule."

"I remember it. I never believed in it."

"We all have our own set of rules."

"That's true. Munro had his too."

"Munro? Who's Munro?"

"Now, take it steady, Tempy," said Goldsmith sympathetically. "It's very easy to forget what you should and shouldn't know. I told you about Munro the other day, remember?"

"Oh *that* fellow. The private eye. Has he been bothering you again?"

"No, not me, Tempy. But he bothered Jennifer, I think, before his accident. He was trying to blackmail her. He had not only collected evidence that Housman was having a bit on the side. He'd also found out the kind of tricks J. T. Hardy's got up to."

"I don't understand a word you're saying. If Munro's a blackmailer, why not tell the police?"

Goldsmith's laughter was ninety-per-cent genuine.

"You do stick with a part, Tempy! Munro's beyond questioning and all the evidence seems happily to have disappeared. And you know what? I shouldn't be at all surprised if it turned out to be not very far away from us here."

"I think you're going a bit funny," said Templewood seriously. "Was that what you turned the house upside down looking for? Jennifer was most distressed. And did you find anything? Clearly not, else you wouldn't need to sit there trying to turn words into facts!"

Goldsmith sipped his drink reflectively. It was difficult to see where to go from here. A gentle tap at the door saved him from immediate decision.

The door was pushed open a couple of feet and Dora's head appeared. Templewood jumped up.

"Hello, what's all this then?" he asked. "Why aren't you in bed, my love? I thought your mum was up there with you?"

"She's in the kitchen making some coffee, I think," said Dora.

"Is she now? And you thought you'd go for a little walk-about, did you? Well, step inside a mo' out of the draught. You know Mr. Goldsmith of course."

"Yes. Hello."

She stepped into the room. She was wearing a pretty blue and yellow night-dress and carrying under her arm an old, battered leather document case. She spoke accusingly to Templewood.

"I was doing some tidying up after Mummy went downstairs and I found this in my secret place at the back of my dolls' house. It's not mine and I wondered if you'd left it there, Uncle Rodney."

Goldsmith beat Templewood by a short head and took the document case from the girl's arm.

"I think it's mine, Dora," he said. "I hope you don't mind, but I hid it there on Saturday. Did you enjoy your swim, by the way?"

"Yes," she said. "I like to swim under water till I think I am drowning, then dive up to the top with a big splash of air."

"Me too," said Goldsmith.

"Now you run along to bed, Dora love, before your mum finds you," said Templewood. "Off you go."

"Just one thing, Dora," said Goldsmith. "Uncle Rodney and I were just trying to remember. How long have you known him?"

She looked at him pensively through her clear grey eyes.

"I think it was just after my last birthday that I really met him for the first time. But I'd seen him sometimes before that."

"And when's your birthday, Dora?"

"February the fifteenth. Nearly Valentine's Day."

"I'll remember that," said Goldsmith. "Good night now."

The girl left and the two men looked at each other, Templewood warily, Goldsmith blankly.

The case was locked.

"Is there a key?" Goldsmith asked.

There was no reply, so he crossed to the bureau, picked up a heavy brass paper-knife and began levering the catch open.

"Jennifer's idea, I should think. Keep all your precious things together. Funny, that was the only room in the house I didn't search. But it must have been your idea to hang on to this stuff. I wonder why? Insurance? There it goes."

The catch gave way. He opened the case. In it were papers, photographs and two rolls of tape. These last he pocketed, glanced cursorily through the rest and thrust them back in the case.

"Well, Uncle Rodney. Do you want to fall on your knees now and confess your sins?"

"Sins?"

"Well, for a start, you didn't get these from Munro as a leaving present, did you?"

"He was a blackmailer," said Templewood with a

shrug. "I found him dead. What did you expect me to do? I grabbed the evidence and left."

"A real stroke of fortune that," said Goldsmith. "But let's start at the beginning. There seem to be two versions of that. One starts, 'One day in September I was walking down Regent Street and I saw this man who looked just like Nikolaus Hebbel.' Now that one's a bit of a fairy tale, I think. The other one begins, 'One day six months ago, or a year ago, or perhaps earlier, I met the wife of this man Housman whom I knew vaguely through my business connections. I turned on the charm, automatically at first, but soon began to realize that I was on to a very good thing indeed." Now to me, Tempy, that one rings true, that has that genuine changing-room stench I associate with you."

"I love the woman," said Templewood with a simple sincerity which might have been touching if Goldsmith had not seen it at work before.

"Lucky her. Now, she wants a divorce. Housman is a bad lot, in more ways than she imagines, perhaps. But you; now you, Tempy, are not so keen. I wonder why? Perhaps you really do fancy her, but if she gets a divorce, what has she got? A big chunk of alimony which may well decrease if she marries again. You're better off with the *status quo*, all the oats you can eat and no rent for the stables."

"Quotation is a subtle form of flattery," said Templewood.

"Is it? Well, in a minute, I'm going to quote what you said to me before the reunion. 'If it's Hebbel, I'll know what to do,' you said. 'You follow him, I'll check up on his home background,' you said. Then off you beat it up the A1 to check on the colour of his bedroom wallpaper. Again."

"All right, Billy. So I knew Housman. But I really did think he could be Hebbel. And, knowing how important this would be to you, I felt I had to let you know. It would just have complicated matters if I'd explained everything. I wanted you to look at him completely unprejudiced."

"It doesn't wash," said Goldsmith wearily. "What you wanted was for Jennifer to be a rich widow with a controlling share in J. T. Hardy's, that's what you wanted."

"You're wrong, Billy," protested Templewood urgently. "He *could* have been Hebbel. Everything fitted. Christ, there's still no proof he wasn't! Is there?"

"Oh yes. I've had Housman's fingerprints checked. I was on the phone to Colonel Maxwell earlier tonight."

Templewood looked genuinely worried.

"Christ, Billy. You were discreet, I hope."

"Very. And you won't be surprised to know that Housman is Housman is Housman. No, Tempy, what you had in mind was a little disposal job. And for some reason you thought of me. Old Billy Goldsmith with whom you discussed the hated Hebbel once a year. Suppose you could convince that well-known gullible fool that Housman was Hebbel? What a weapon you would have created!"

"And that's where your theories fall to bits, Billy," said Templewood. "If you recall, when I saw you at the reunion, I told you that I'd found nothing to support the identification and I remember I even apologized for wasting your time. What happened after that you did off your own bat and it took me absolutely by surprise, I tell you!"

"I'm sure, I'm sure," agreed Goldsmith. "I've been thinking about that. Yes, you're quite right, you did change your tune, didn't you? If my theory was right, then you'd have come back with some bits of incontrovertible evidence that it was Hebbel."

"Right," said Templewood. "So bang goes your crazy idea. Let's have another drink."

"But suppose," said Goldsmith ignoring him, "suppose that when you came north for those two days, Jennifer confided in you that despite your advice to the contrary, she'd hired a detective. And that at that very moment he was following her husband around London, collecting evidence, wouldn't *that* give you pause? You must have realized what a near squeak you'd had. All this build-up to killing Housman, and a trained eye was watching over him all the time! No wonder you cooled things down when you came back!"

"No wonder you're in politics, Billy," said Templewood admiringly. "You can make yourself believe your own fantasies! What was I going to do—get you to slip a cobra into his pyjamas? Or a bomb in his car perhaps?"

Now Goldsmith helped himself to another drink.

"No," he answered. "Not quite. I've been thinking about that. I mean, why me? You're an ingenious fellow. And I know from experience that you don't value other people's lives very highly. But why involve me? I puzzled about it as I drove down here tonight. Nearly had a crash because my mind wasn't on my driving. And then I think I got it."

"Keep taking the tablets," said Templewood halfheartedly. "And no alcohol, mind."

"You must have wanted me for a special reason. I mean, why think of Hebbel at all? You must have thought of me first. So there had to be a connection between me and Housman, and the other day I saw it. In fact I mentioned it to you the first time you mentioned J. T. Hardy's. They hire from us. Housman himself was due to be picked up at Leeds airport on his return from London. You knew Harewood Hire-Cars had the job. Perhaps Jennifer had mentioned it, or Housman himself. And instantly it clicked. What did you have in mind, Uncle Rodney? Mechanical failure? Or me leaving the back-end of a limousine across a railway line? Perhaps I was to bash him over the head first and hope it would able put down to the crash? Whatever happened you'd be out of sight. And Housman would be dead before he could be so inconveniently divorced. A simple accident. Simple as stumbling and falling into the electric fire. Only you found out how to do that one by yourself, didn't you, Tempy? Or you found yourself another partner."

The suggestion evoked no answer. Templewood merely sighed deeply and leaned back in his chair, staring sightlessly at the ceiling.

"You're not going to go round proclaiming these daft ideas, are you?" he asked finally.

"That depends on what you're going to do."

Templewood stood up slowly, shaking his head as if in disbelief.

"Billy, Billy," he said. "What are you trying to do? You're doing the knight-errant bit, but there's no one to protect. Only us. Is it Jennifer that's bothering you? All right, so she's made a big impression, but she's no babe in the wood. Christ, man, a couple of minutes ago you were suggesting that she might be my partner in crime! Well that's nonsense, there was no crime. But she's certainly been my partner in other things, and very willing and enthusiastic too. Don't get angry, please, Billy. You've no claim on her, don't you see that?"

"Or is it Dora? Look, with me for a dad, she'll get a better deal than she could have hoped for from that randy old fiddler with all his kinks and quirks. I like the kid, she likes me, you've seen it.

"So who're you protecting, Billy? Or who are you attacking, perhaps that's more important. Is it me you're after? Are you jealous perhaps? You've no right to be, Billy boy. What have I done to you?"

Now Goldsmith rose too and the two men faced each other, Goldsmith's face twisted in such anger that Templewood uneasily backed away.

"What have you done?" he echoed. "You've made me a killer, that's all."

Templewood halted his retreat, raised his bushy eyebrows in amazement, then threw back his head and roared with laughter.

"Billy, oh Billy! A killer. *I've* made you a killer! Oh no. You've forgotten where this all really started, haven't you? Just for a moment, you're really seeing yourself as the injured innocent! You've managed to forget Hebbel."

"I don't care about Hebbel," said Goldsmith. "It doesn't bother me. I'll be glad to get it out of the way. It doesn't bother me!"

But even to his own ears, his protestation had the stridency which accompanies lack of conviction.

"Of course it bothers you," said Templewood, now quite back in the ascendancy. "It's me it doesn't bother. It never did really. But it bothers you. I've always known that; every year at the reunion, I've gone out of my way to make it keep on bothering you. It amused me and you never know when it might come in useful, knowing how to get to a man. Well, it's come in useful, hasn't it? So just think; you open your mouth and it won't be just a case of Jennifer knowing you killed her husband and Dora knowing you killed her dad; they'll both know, and everyone will know, that the reason Billy Goldsmith survived the dreadful deprivations and tortures of captivity was because he collaborated, and the reason he was so eager to rid the world of Hebbel, was that dear Nikolaus, if caught, would testify as damningly against Goldsmith as the other way around!"

There it was. The words had been spoken. The cause of his agitation of mind and spirit for nearly two decades had been given voice. It came as a cue, and he spoke the defence he had rehearsed in his mind unconsciously for all those years.

"You led me into it. We told him nothing important. We *knew* nothing important. It was a survival technique, that was all."

"Of course it was. And we *did* survive. The other seven didn't though, did they? Nor would we have done if that air attack hadn't scattered that SS regiment. Then those bloody Frenchmen talked and got us elected as star witnesses. Now, I think we were justified, Billy boy. I'll stand up and tell the world so. We'll face them together, you and I, Billy boy. Then off to Acapulco till things quieten down."

"It'd be your word against mine," said Goldsmith,

trying to collect himself. "Which would they believe, I wonder."

"The worst. Who ever believes anything else? And it's not just me, is it? Somewhere out there, dear old Nikolaus is lurking. You can never tell when he'll be turned up, can you? This boy Wiesenthal in Vienna, he doesn't go to sleep at night unless he's caught at least two war criminals since breakfast. Well, if you want to forestall him, off you go and tell your story. If you want everyone in the country to think your name stinks, pick up the telephone. If you want everyone you've ever liked or respected to give you the fisheye, then start confessing. You confess for me, and I'll confess for you."

Templewood did not mean it, but he was offering Goldsmith a genuine temptation. A single act of atonement, a once-for-all confession and remittance, this was what most men desired. If it could be simple, clear-cut . . . but the original act had appeared simple and clear-cut, and so had so many choices, ill and good, made since then.

Templewood broke into his train of thought once more.

"I think you'll see things right, Billy. You're more like me than you care to imagine. Don't worry about these two girls. They'll have a good life with me. I'll be your prototype dad, strict but kind. And Jennifer'll need never worry about me fishing in someone else's pond. I'm too fly to get caught! Meanwhile, you'll go on to bigger and better things. We can be useful to each other, Billy boy. Me in business, you in public life."

Goldsmith smiled humourlessly.

"That's a weak lever you're applying, Tempy. There's no way for me to get selected after my performance on Saturday. Christ knows how I got into the last three."

Templewood roared with laughter.

"Why, Billy, if that's all that's bothering you, relax. You've got powerful friends."

"What do you mean?"

Templewood reached over for Munro's case and patted it affectionately.

"I got hold of this on Thursday evening. (That's when I found Munro dead, poor fellow.) I did a quick study of it and, well, as you can imagine it was very interesting stuff. Worth hanging on to. Now I remembered what you said about the Selection Board, I don't forget old friends, and I chatted with a couple of people on Friday . . ."

"Who, for God's sake?" demanded Goldsmith.

"Well, there's a nice old boy called Edmunds, for one . . ."

*"Edmunds!* You mean Edmunds is mixed up in this J. T. Hardy's business?"

Templewood tapped his nose significantly.

"We just had a chat. I explained I was likely very soon to be a man of some importance at J. T. Hardy's and hoped his policy of co-operation with the company would continue. He was very interested. I mentioned your name as a personal friend of mine, just in passing. I hope you don't mind."

"But the police . . . Christ! No wonder that old hypocrite was interested in what Vickers had been saying."

"The police have been whistling in the dark. You gave them a tune to have a go at for a while, but it's over the hills and far away now. So, what do you say, Billy? I wouldn't be surprised if Edmunds weren't trying to get hold of you at this very moment. How about a future full of mutual goodwill and co-operation? Comrades once and comrades ever!"

They sat and looked at each other for a long twenty seconds. Then Goldsmith turned his gaze aside and peered into the fireplace. The house was quite still. No outside noise penetrated into this room and neither of its occupants moved.

Greenmansion would be Templewood's, thought Goldsmith. And all that belonged in it. J. T. Hardy's would be Templewood's too and all that belonged there. He would be a man of widespread and various

properties. And Templewood's properties would be
kept in good repair, there was no doubt of that.

It would be easy to destroy him now. No, he corrected
himself; not all that easy, and *destroy* was the wrong
word. Destruction was not a sudden thing, though it
might seem like it. Destruction could take ten, twenty
years. A lifetime perhaps. And something might still
be left intact.

"Have you made up your mind, Billy boy?" asked
Templewood in a kind voice.

Before he could reply, the door opened and Jennifer entered with a tray.

"I've made some coffee," she said.

He watched her placing it on the table, her delicately-
boned head bowed low, while Templewood stood beside her looking down with a benevolent smile on his
face.

"We've just been talking about the future," he said.
"Bill here's hoping to get into Parliament."

"Is he?"

She looked at him with a mild interest. At least
some of her former distaste seemed to have evaporated. Perhaps Templewood had sent out some signal
of approval. She would be a good wife for the public
occasion. And for the private, now he would never
know.

"I've just been listening to a radio programme," she
continued. "They all seem to think it will be Butler.
And a general election in the spring. What do you
think, Mr. Goldsmith?"

Me, I know nothing, he thought. I know nothing
about this woman, or her dead husband, or what
Templewood is thinking, or how Munro died. All I
know is what I am.

"They're all wrong, my love," interjected Templewood. "It'll be Home."

"Who?" she said.

"The noble lord. I know how their minds work.
And they'll hang on till next September, October even.
You wait and see. What say you, Billy? Soon enough,
I think. You'll be well established as the candidate

by then, and autumn's always been a good time for
you."

    I can't do it, thought Goldsmith. I must speak now.

    Templewood picked up his coffee-cup.

    "Here's to the future," he said.

    And holding the cup high before him, he waited for
the others to join in the toast.

# PART TWO
## 1970

# CHAPTER I

"AND IN CONCLUSION," said the speaker, "if the last six years have shown nothing else, they have surely proved that it is possible for a Labour government and the world of business and commerce to work hand in hand for the mutual benefit of the people and the nation."

He sat down to applause that was polite rather than enthusiastic, though to his finely tuned ear it sounded rather more prolonged than the reception given to his speech on the same occasion the previous year.

"Fine speech, Minister," puffed a cigar-clouded face to his left, while the gross figure to his right applauded by beating one hand on the table in order that the other could keep his brandy almost constantly at his lips.

Bastards, thought Goldsmith as he nodded in reply. They can afford to make a bit more noise now they think they'll be rid of us in a six month.

Afterwards as he chatted to his luncheon hosts, concealing his impatience at the time it was taking for his car to arrive, he heard a familiar voice and someone touched his arm.

"Minister, how are you?" said Templewood with a large grin. "It's good to see you again."

Goldsmith looked at him blankly for a second.

"Templewood. J. T. Hardy's," murmured a helpful aide. "Lunching with you tomorrow."

"Of course. Mr. Templewood, how do you do?"

They shook hands.

"The Minister's car's here," said a distant voice.

As he walked down the stairs, he found Templewood had contrived to be at his elbow.

"You're a cagey one," he muttered admiringly.

"It's necessary," smiled Goldsmith.

"See you tomorrow."

The official car swept smoothly into the stream of traffic and bore him sedately towards Westminster. He glanced at his watch. It was nearly four p.m. He groaned.

His aide smiled sympathetically.

"The more insignificant the occasion, the longer the luncheon," he said knowingly.

"And the more minor the main guest?" added Goldsmith ironically.

"No, I didn't mean that," said the other, unperturbed.

"That's good."

He looked at his watch again.

"Something special you're late for, sir?"

"No. Not really. Just some of the electorate on a day trip. I promised them a guided tour, then tea. Starting at three."

"With a bit of luck, they may not have waited."

But of course they had.

"Liz, Mrs. Sewell. Sorry I'm late, but I had to listen to myself making a speech."

"That's all right, Bill. We needed a sit down. Mam's half killed me, dragging me round the shops."

The passing years hadn't changed Liz much. She was a bit solider now, her face was a little more lined, but she looked as healthy and energetic as ever and her hair poured mockingly out of the tight bun in which she had attempted to restrain it.

"How's Jeff?" Goldsmith asked.

"Oh, he's fine. Sends his regards."

Later while Liz had gone wandering off in search of a loo, he asked her mother, "How is she?"

"Drop the hushed concern, Bill," said Mrs. Sewell, lighting her ninth or tenth cigarette. "She's fine. Not that that little creep can give her what you could. He's a bystander, that one. I always said it. Hell, he brings me a cup of tea in the mornings just so he can have a peek at my tits."

Goldsmith laughed. Strangely, one result of his final break with Liz and her marriage two years later to Malleson had been a much easier relationship with her mother.

"You're still living with them then."

"Too true," she said firmly. "None of this *I'll be no bother, just put me in a home* cant for me. I'm too old to change my ways."

"Quite right," agreed Goldsmith with the certainty of the uninvolved.

"There hasn't been all that much change here since the Red Army marched in either," said Mrs. Sewell, eyeing him with a touch of malice.

"No. Less than we hoped," he answered glumly. "Not to worry. I dare say we'll soon be marching out again."

Mrs. Sewell looked alarmed.

"For Christ's sake, don't let our Liz hear you talk like that. I don't know what's happening down here, but up in Yorkshire the revolution's still just round the corner. I mean the kind of revolution that'll have everybody reading the *Guardian* instead of the *Sun.*"

They laughed together as Liz returned. Her mother rose.

"I'll try my luck," she said. "It's a kind of contact with the great."

They watched her move away.

"Remarkable woman," observed Goldsmith.

"You used to think she was a pain in the arse."

"Opinions change," he said.

"So do arses. You happy, Bill?"

"I think so."

"You've done well for yourself."

He shrugged.

"I just happened to be handy during the last shuffle. Next time trumps might change and I'll be out."

"No," she contradicted him vigorously. "Anyway, let's change the subject. When we see you at home, all we ever talk about is politics. How's your love life?"

"So so," he answered vaguely. "There's not much time."

"Get on! One of the big shots at work reckoned he saw you with some smart young dolly-bird last time he was in town."

"Up for t' Cup?" said Goldsmith with a smile. "It was probably the Japanese Ambassador in a bad light."

He glanced at his watch.

"Visiting time up already?" asked Liz.

"I'm afraid so. It's my fault for being late. Still, I'll be up the weekend after next, so I'll see you and Jeff then. How's old Edmunds by the way? This last attack sounded a bad one."

"Oh Bill, I forgot all about it, it's been such a rush. But he's dead. We got the news just as we were leaving for the train this morning. I'm sure they'll have rung your office since."

"Ay, I'm sure," he said. "It'll be waiting in my In-tray. It should be in the other, properly speaking. Well, so the old bastard's gone! That'll mean I'll be up earlier than I thought. I'll be looked for at the funeral."

"Bill!" Liz protested. "Is that all it means to you, another trip? He had his faults, I know, but he did a lot for the town in his time. And he was a good friend to you on the Selection Board."

"Yes, yes. You're right there," said Goldsmith reflectively. "He certainly was."


It was after ten o'clock when he got back to his flat that night. As he parked his car, a figure rose from a semi-recumbent position in a nearby Mercedes and wound down the window.

He walked over to her.

"It's worse than being married to a shift-worker," she yawned.

"The difference is, Sandra," he answered, "you're not married and you get paid for waiting time. Come on up."

Six years had touched Sandra Phillips even less than

it had Liz. Her exact age was still a mystery to him. Their relationship was a good, solid, business one which suited him very well, though he still remembered with a sensuous nostalgia the free introductory offer he had sampled in the twenty-four hours following his arrival on her doorstep with the Munro tapes in his hand.

"Why can't you either be on time, or come to my place, or let me have a key to yours?"

"Security," he said.

"What do you mean, security?" she asked indignantly.

"I mean Special Branch have got their gear set up at my place tonight and I've sold all the tickets. We can't disappoint them."

The phone was ringing as he entered.

"Goldsmith," he said.

"Hello," said the caller. "Sorry to trouble you, sir, but I just wondered if you'd heard the sad news about Mr. Edmunds."

"Yes, yes. I had. I'm very distressed. He was a good man."

"He'll be very much missed," said the caller. "Hard to replace."

"It'll need thought."

"It will. Well, sorry to have troubled you. Good night."

"Good night."

So, he thought as he replaced the receiver, Templewood was worried. Good. It was nice to think of Templewood being worried.

"I suppose it's an advantage in a way," said Sandra as she undressed.

"What is?"

"Specializing in security-minded politicians. Everything's so marvellously discreet. Though it can go too far. After poor old Profumo, you'd have thought that every time they had an erection a red light flashed on at Scotland Yard. But now, they are just very careful. Mind, you're the carefullest of all. That's why you stick to me and me alone, I think. Safety in lack of numbers."

"I've never cared for orgies. It's one of the disadvantages of not having a public-school education. I hope you pick nice discreet girls for my colleagues?"

"I do my best, but things aren't what they used to be. Why do you ask, Bill? You're not beginning to hanker after a younger vintage, are you? Or two or three?"

"Not particularly," he answered, carefully hanging his suit in the wardrobe.

"I thought I saw you a couple of weeks ago with a young thing in tow," she said casually. "Is she not coming across then?"

"My niece probably," he said calmly.

"Really?" she said with light disbelief. "Come to Auntie."

"These have been good years, Billy. Bloody good years."

Templewood leaned back in his chair and sighed with retrospective satisfaction.

"Yes," said Goldsmith.

Templewood had been one of a small party of businessmen he had entertained to lunch in the House and he had contrived to be the last to leave.

"We're big now. Very big. Another year, who knows? J. T. Hardy's International. How does that sound?"

"You've done wonders, Tempy."

"But you can't mark time, Billy. And you've got to remember your roots. Now, Edmunds is going to be a miss."

"Yes. Thanks for ringing."

"I thought you'd like to know. Now, I've got a couple of prospects for his replacement. No one with his kind of contacts and authority yet, of course. That's why I wanted to consult you. Which of these two do you think's the best bet?"

He mentioned two names.

"They've both nibbled, have they?" asked Goldsmith.

"Naturally. One's had a couple of consultancy fees. The other took a trip to Ibiza at our expense last year.

But the next step's the big one. You know where you are then, no more self-deception."

"Yes, I know the step. Give me a bit of time to think about it. I'll let you know."

"That's fine. You'll be going up to the funeral? Give you a chance to hear what the talk is."

"True." Goldsmith finished his drink and looked impatiently at his watch for the benefit of any spectators. An MP trapped by an influential and overfed guest was a common enough sight.

"How's Jennifer?" he asked.

"Fine, fine," Templewood said. "Er, she said that Dora mentioned you in one of her letters. You've seen her then? She didn't mention it when I looked her up last week."

"Oh yes. Now that she's studying at the University here, I thought I should keep an avuncular eye on her," said Goldsmith blandly.

"Avuncular, is it?" said Templewood. "Well, no funny stuff, mind. Not with Dora."

"It would bother you? Strange. Well, never fear, Tempy. You know I'm the soul of honour."

"So you tell me. Well, I'd better be off."

"Making another million for us?"

"Not this afternoon," Templewood grinned. "No, I met this khaki bird at some wog reception last week. She wears a blonde wig. Jesus, you should see her. It makes you understand Livingstone."

"Be careful," said Goldsmith. "Remember Munro."

Templewood paused half out of his chair and looked quizzically at his host.

"I remember him," he said. "And he got sorted out all right, didn't he? Watch how you vote, Billy. See you."

Goldsmith stood up and watched him go, stifling back a yawn. As he made for the door himself, he caught the eye of his opposite number on the Opposition benches who smiled sympathetically. They knew each other well.

"I've got the same lot next week," he said.

"Serves you right. They're the price of capitalism," answered Goldsmith.

"He makes a lot of jobs for a lot of people," replied the other in a Pavlovian reflex that was quite without heat.

"Yes, he does," agreed Goldsmith. "He does."

The same afternoon he had another guest for tea. It was Dora Housman. At nineteen she had all her mother's neat elegance and self-containment, but matched with a vivacity whose visible symbol might have been the golden hair which poured down over her shoulders.

"Hi," she said.

"Hello. How's the work?"

"It stinks."

"Be precise."

"I thought that because I like books, reading English would be my thing. But all the time, it seems to be about coming at it from such odd angles."

"Doesn't it sometimes improve the sensation when you get there?"

"Does it? I don't know. I think the thing is I'm no scholar and I don't fancy three years going through the motions."

"What do you fancy, Dora?"

He smiled at her affectionately, conscientiously playing the uncle.

"I'm not sure. There's nothing for me in the university world, not at the moment. Perhaps I'd like to write, but everyone says that, don't they?"

"Will you go back north?"

She opened the cool, grey eyes wide.

"You're joking! No, I'll stop here and serve in a shop if necessary. You said something last week when you took me out to dinner. Something about a job. Were you serious?"

"If you are."

"I'm not sure. Can we talk about it?"

"Certainly," he said. "Perhaps we could have dinner again."

She played with her long hair, curling it into ringlets, and looked at him speculatively.

"How's your mother?" he asked.

"She seems fine. Just the same, only more so."

"And your step-father?"

"Oh, Rodney. No change there either. He's down here at the moment, did you know? Bought me a lunch on Monday. I took a girl-friend along, thought I might as well squeeze as much as poss for the worthy needy from him. He was a bit annoyed at first, I think, but after the soup, he was gazing deep, deep into her peerless eyes and sending out the bedroom signals."

"Did she answer?"

"I don't know. I gave her my blessing—and warning— afterwards. They're both human beings."

She pulled her hair out straight once more and gazed assessingly directly into Goldsmith's face.

"Talking of which and such, I mean, where is all this taking us?"

"I'm sorry?"

"I mean, it's all very flattering and so on to be wined and dined by a big, important politician . . ."

"A very junior Minister," he corrected.

". . . but you're nobody's uncle, Bill. That's why I liked you when you first came round, I think. You made such a rotten job of the uncle bit that I could see someone real inside. So where are we going?"

"God knows," he said, "and he's not going to tell us. We all end up doing things, *being* things, that none of us could have foreseen. You can make plans, have visions, but something gets in the way. And generally speaking, when you look at the obstacle closely, it might be disguised as a war, or an accident, or a duty, but it's only yourself."

"My God," she said. "If that rhymed it could have been by Patience Strong. Or even Mary Wilson."

"Hush," he said, grinning. "I'm forty-five tomorrow, put it down to that. Why not join me in a little birthday dinner and we'll try to find out where we're going from there? But don't come if you want to stay safe with Super-Uncle. And I'll see about the job either way. No strings. What do you say?"

She took hold of her hair again and pulled it across

her face till only the grey eyes, momentarily blank, were visible.

Then, "All right," she said.

He relaxed in his chair and poured himself another cup of tea.

"Forty-five," he said. "You know, I don't think I've ever looked forward to a birthday so much."

# CHAPTER II

HE AWOKE EARLY the following morning and was seated in his office by seven-thirty. He spent an hour meticulously checking through a file marked J. T. Hardy's. In it were records of all his contacts, official and unofficial, with the firm over the past six years. He had similar files on half-a-dozen other large concerns; merely to have concentrated on one would have been a way of causing suspicion rather than removing it. They all contained evidence of his scrupulous refusal to accept anything which might be construed as a form of inducement. On occasions he had permitted himself to keep, say, a single bottle of brandy or box of cigars. It was important to appear as a human being rather than a moral stone-wall. But the return or disposal of larger gifts was carefully documented.

The difference between the J. T. Hardy's file and the others was that the former contained a great deal more and that much of the documentary evidence of rejection in it was fraudulent.

It had been a difficult task and had become progressively more difficult as his career went into its dramatic up-swing three years earlier. Templewood's pressures on him for advice, assistance and influence had also increased, and though whenever possible he refused reward, Templewood was astute enough to realize that the first job of the corrupter is to get those involved to step in so deeply that there can be no going back. So the consultancy fees, the gifts, the hospitality offers had rained down.

The money problem he had dealt with by apparently
playing into Templewood's hands and refusing to accept unrecorded payments in cash. To explain away
accepting several thousand pounds wrapped in a brown
paper parcel handed over in a cinema would be an
impossible task. But "consultancy fees" appeared on
balance sheets and the progress of the money could be
easily checked. The file contained (as did all the files
where consultancy fees had been paid) a carbon of a
letter in which Goldsmith reminded the firm's officials
that he had expressed his unwillingness to accept any
fee but had agreed to do so on the understanding that
he would not retain the monies but pass them on to
one of a number of registered charities.

Each file contained certified receipts from a variety
of charities for the total amount received.

In the case of J. T. Hardy's the letter had never been
sent, but the carbon was there and the receipts were
genuine. If the absence of the letter from the company's own records was ever noticed, it would only be in
circumstances where this would reflect very badly on
the integrity of its executives.

Similarly with gifts; according to Goldsmith's records, everything had been returned or occasionally
passed on. A letter from a Community Welfare Group
in his own constituency described with a mixture of
gratitude and awe the difference his gift of six cases of
malt whisky had made to their Pensioners' Christmas
Party. One local Meals-on-Wheels group were happily
using a Royal Doulton dinner service, and the few
people who ever asked for a cup of coffee at the
Trades and Labour Club were likely to have it poured
out of a Georgian silver coffee-pot.

Templewood had been far from pleased and very
close to suspicion when he had read about Goldsmith's
generosity in sending a retired miner and his wife on
an all-expenses-paid luxury holiday in the Canaries,
but had accepted Goldsmith's explanation that he preferred to arrange his own dirty week-ends on a much
more discreet scale. It was an argument which ap-
pealed to the Templewood philosophy.

Templewood was also amused and impressed by the assiduity with which Goldsmith supported the demands for a register of MPs' business interests. "Like a tart demanding an examination to prove she's still got her maidenhead," he described it, adding seriously, "and it works, because most of the others are tarts too and the last thing they want is a bloody doctor in the House!"

So for six years, Goldsmith had aided and abetted Templewood in developing J. T. Hardy's into the huge concern it had become. He had in the process become a businessman, and in a sense it was the public effects in speech and debate of this undercover activity which had brought him to the notice of the party hierarchy and eventually to his present lowly eminence.

But initially it was for his own protection that the expertise had been acquired; and with his acquisition of influence and authority, so enthusiastically welcomed by Templewood, he had come to realize that what he could help create, he could help destroy. His file had at first merely been an insurance; now it became the cornerstone of a defence case which no one else yet knew was going to have to be made.

During his association with J. T. Hardy's, he had talked to no one except Templewood himself, and he had avoided writing any letters other than those he was willing to go on public record. There was no way of checking what Templewood might have said to any of his associates about his connections at Westminster; he was the kind of man who might not have been able to resist the boastful hint; but hearsay was no evidence. Only one other man existed who could significantly involve Goldsmith in a corruption scandal, and that was the man whose influence and authority had got him adopted as the Party candidate.

Edmunds.

And now Edmunds was dead.

So now it could begin.

J. T. Hardy's and all its subsidiaries were slightly overstretched. Templewood's eagerness for expansion had always been accompanied by this danger and Gold-smith had done what he could to encourage it. It was not that there was much obvious cause for concern, merely that at the moment, the company was relying a little too heavily on confidence and a little too lightly on capital. Such moments, Goldsmith had come to realize, occurred in the lives of all flourishing busi-nesses. If you leap forward, there has to be a time when both feet are off the ground. There was no reason in the world for concern.

Unless the confidence the business world felt in the firm could be undermined.

He opened his appointments book and looked through the list of his engagements that day.

There was a tap on his door and Jenkinson, his private secretary came in.

"Morning, sir," he said briskly. "And a Happy Birth-day to you."

"You remembered," answered Goldsmith. "But then you've had a long time lying in bed to brood on the events of the day, haven't you?"

Jenkinson looked pained. It was just eight-thirty a.m.

"It looks fairly busy today, but I'd like to fit Tranter from the Board of Trade in somewhere. Just a chat. See what you can do."

"Yes, sir. I'll try. It *is* a busy day. Now tonight . . ."

"Tonight I'm going out to dinner. It *is* my birthday, after all. Get Miss Alcott to book me a table at the Peacock. Eight-thirty. For two."

He gave other instructions, Jenkinson disappeared and returned half an hour later like a spaniel with a stick to announce all had been done as requested.

"And I've fitted Tranter in at three o'clock," he concluded.

"Fine. That's fine."

This was the way to start things. Nothing in writing; a quiet word expressing vague concern about certain rumours which had reached him from his constituency about the way in which J. T. Hardy's were conducting their business; reluctance to speak—personal knowl-

edge of many of the people concerned in the business—
but duty was duty; and he dimly recollected there had
been some police interest in the firm six, seven years
ago . . .

So the mills would start grinding.

And next would come a few words in the financial
and business world. Interest being shown in J. T.
Hardy's—no, not an investigation exactly, but . . .

It was a downward spiral and the first curves would
be so wide-sweeping and so gently inclined that they
would hardly be perceptible. The bottom was months,
perhaps even years away and by the time it was reached,
the starting point would be untraceable.

In the early stages, however, there was always the
chance that a perceptive and resourceful man could
grab the sides and hang on. But he would need all his
wits about him and all his energy concentrated in one
direction.

Goldsmith smiled humourlessly at the thought of
another file he had been compiling. This one he kept
in the safe in his flat. It contained enough evidence
of Templewood's many adulteries to win a dozen di-
vorces. Goldsmith knew Jennifer well enough to believe that with this in her possession, she would not
hesitate to start proceedings. She was a woman who
could live with suspicions if she chose to, but who
would refuse to close her eyes to the truth. And
Templewood was a man who despite his many infideli-
ties retained a disproportionate pride in his elegant
wife and home.

So if he grabbed the sides, thought Goldsmith, this
will prise the bastard loose.

There was another reason why he would like to see
a divorce between Jennifer and Templewood.

Dora.

He shifted uneasily in his seat at the thought of her.
Only in this area did he find his motives at all ambiguous. With Templewood he was paying off an old score,
one which went back to the beginnings of their acquaintance. If there were any external object from

which all that was undignified, and culpable, and rotten in his life stemmed, it was Templewood. He could even, were he so inclined, argue that by disposing of Templewood, he was doing a public service by fitting himself better to carry out the duties of his office. But he rarely claimed in his internal debates motives so altruistic.

Jennifer he felt nothing for now. Templewood had had her before he met her, had enjoyed her for the past six years. To the world at large she still appeared the same elegant, delicate beauty she had always been. To Goldsmith she was irrecoverably tarnished.

Dora was different. Her childhood affection for "Uncle Rodney" had been replaced by that most devastating of attitudes, total comprehension without moral judgment. The real enemy of the immoral is the amoral; and Templewood, deprived of his ability either to shock or to justify himself, was at a loss. With any other woman, his answer would have been to go into his seduction routine, but he had established a relationship with Dora which made this impossible for him.

But not for Goldsmith. Tonight he might well end up in bed with Dora and he was not sure why.

It would be the most devastating blow of all to Templewood. It would perhaps at last surprise Jennifer. But what it would mean to himself he was not clear. Or to Dora, for that matter.

Could he marry her? He had no idea how she would react to the suggestion. But the vaguest possibility of this happening made it essential that her mother should divorce Templewood. Otherwise the connection would be uncomfortably close when the J. T. Hardy's affair finally broke.

Love should be the touchstone, he supposed. He examined his feelings and found them ambivalent. He liked the girl but did not wholly understand her. As for simple, uncomplicated affection and friendship, he probably had rather more of that in his relationship with Sandra Phillips.

But that too would have to come to an end, he had decided. He had been careful there, but care in such matters could only take you so far. More out of curiosity than with any particular plan in mind, he had made copies of the Munro tapes before returning the originals to Sandra. One at least of the voices he had recognized and over the years he had amused himself by uncovering the identities of Sandra's other political customers. By now he had a fair idea of their habits and predilections, some of which he found distasteful, but it was their lack of discretion which distressed him most. If (and he admitted to himself privately the chances were high) the Tories were returned to power at the next election, one or more of these men might achieve positions of high responsibility. Then the information he possessed would possibly come in very useful. They would deserve anything they got.

And it was at this point in his reasoning that he had considered the vulnerability of his own position. Since then his meetings with Sandra had become rarer and even more circumspect. He trusted her, but he recalled that Munro had got himself into a position from which he could bring pressure to bear on her. There were cleverer men than Munro in the world.

No, it would have to end. But not violently, not too suddenly.

He found that he had risen and was standing staring down out of his window. There was nothing to see below, only parked cars, but suddenly he thought of the attic room in Greenmansion and the papered alcoves. Which of the windows would Dora choose to stand at after she had been in his bed that night?

He shook his head with a sigh and went back to work. The machine had been started. He was what he was. Nothing could stop things now.

At nine-thirty the telephone rang.

"A Brigadier Maxwell. From the War Office."

"What? Oh yes. Put him through, Miss Alcott."

"Goldsmith? Hello, there. Maxwell here."

"Hello, Colonel; sorry, Brigadier. Congratulations."

Don't bother, my boy. It's a sop before they chuck me out. Look, I'm sorry to trouble you, know you're a busy man destroying the Army and all that . . ."

Goldsmith tried to interrupt with a Party-like disclaimer, but Maxwell brushed him aside.

". . . but I thought you would like to know. Just heard this very minute; at long last they've picked up Hebbel."

It was like standing on the long ridge behind his cottage once more, looking up into the cloud-black sky and seeing the dead branch tumbling towards him from the wind-shaken tree. This time, he could not move.

"Hello. Hello! You still there, Goldsmith?"

"Yes."

"Good. Thought I'd lost you for a moment. Well, as I say, the news just came through. No details, except that they took him in Germany last night."

"It's a positive identification, is it?" asked Goldsmith with a steadiness he felt quite proud of.

"Yes, I believe so. The Jewish Documentation Centre in Vienna, Wiesenthal's lot, they picked up the trail and they don't make mistakes. They got him by chance, it seems, while they were after someone else. As you know, he's not very high on their own lists; no, he's one of the few who's peculiarly ours. But it'll create a stir, I should think. British Minister as principal witness and all that. Templewood too. He's a big name now. Thought you should know before the newsmen sniff it out."

"Yes. Many thanks," said Goldsmith. "I'm very grateful. You'll keep me posted?"

"Of course. Goodbye now."

So. When man works everything out, fate produces the unimaginable.

Well, it didn't matter, of course. There would be a courtroom somewhere; photographs, television, interviews, and finally he would stand up and look at

Hebbel (how old now? only in his fifties, still alert and lively) and answer the questions. There would be questions from Hebbels's counsel too, perhaps from Hebbel himself, and they would try to drag the truth of the matter from him. Not that it made Hebbel any the less guilty, but if his evidence could be discredited, if the world could be made to see that this so-called English hero had, without being touched let alone tortured, told everything he knew, even indicating which of his captured comrades were holding back useful information, then any evidence he might offer about the killing of these same comrades, that must be discredited too.

But it didn't matter, he repeated to himself. No one was going to take notice of a Nazi war-criminal desperately seeking to wriggle off the hook. And he mustn't forget Templewood. They were two to one. They had long ago rehearsed their version to perfection. Before the pair of them, Hebbel would have no chance of being believed. No, Templewood would be too much for the German. With Templewood's support, he could bluff this whole thing out and come through to the other side with his reputation untouched or perhaps even enhanced.

He reached for the telephone. Templewood was probably still in London. He would have to be warned, then they would have to meet and discuss tactics. He found himself longing for the man's hearty reassurances, his self-confidence, his Machiavellian expertise.

But he did not touch the phone. For a moment it was as if he did not need to, Templewood's presence in his mind was so strong. Then it vanished like a thread of smoke and he sat back in his chair, feeling exhausted.

Templewood was no refuge, he told himself. All his life, it seemed, he had been dancing around the man as he pulled strings and pressed levers. This very morning he had been congratulating himself on finally facing up to him and challenging his supremacy. But

even the challenge had been cast down in the kind of
oblique, subtle, ambiguous way which was Templewood's own. He planned to destroy him secretly, to
strike out of darkness and from behind.

He rose and began to pace around the room with
growing excitement. Once before he had sensed the
temptation of confession and atonement but had successfully resisted. This time, however, this time . . .
there must be nothing histrionic, nothing self-indulgent.
He was no martyr, had no desire to end up in jail. But
he could refuse to testify on the grounds that his
action at the time and the quarter-century of decep-
tion which had followed made him incompetent. He
would return his medal, given for the terror-controlled
actions of fifteen minutes while others had stoically
endured five years of war for nothing.

And he would, of course, resign from this political
life, which contained so much and demanded so much
which he felt alien and repugnant to his true inner
being. The old escape route was still open. There were
still empty areas in this country where a man could
settle alone and free from the pollution of society.

He sat for nearly an hour letting image upon image
of this new life pile up in his mind till it seemed so real
and tangible that he just had to step through his office
door to find it. The arrival of Jenkinson to remind him
of his first appointment scarcely disturbed his reverie
and the young man was beginning to look quite worried before Goldsmith finally took notice of him.

"Jenkinson," he said. "Just the man."

"Sir?" said Jenkinson. "It's ten-thirty. There's a lot
to be done this morning."

"More than you think," said Goldsmith, feeling
lightheaded, almost tipsy. "First I want to see the PM
as soon as possible. It's urgent. See what you can fix.
After that, cancel my meeting with Tranter, in fact
cancel all my engagements. Including my dinner tonight. Get a message through to Miss Dora Housman
at Birkbeck College and say I regret but I've got to go
away unexpectedly."

"Sir?" said Jenkinson in puzzlement. Goldsmith ignored him.

". . . and don't hang around."

"Sir."

Jenkinson made for the door, but Goldsmith called him back.

"And Jenkinson, dump this in the destructor, will you?"

He handed over his J. T. Hardy's file. The other files he kept at home could go into the fire that night.

He waited till the door closed behind the young man and reached for the phone. Now he could deal with Templewood, give him the news, tell him of his decision. Let him make of it what he could. Now he felt untouchable.

But the telephone rang as his hand closed on the receiver.

"I have Brigadier Maxwell on the line again, sir."

He hesitated then steeled himself. He had to start somewhere and it might as well be with Maxwell.

"All right. Put him through."

"Goldsmith, it's me again, I'm afraid. Sooner than I expected, but we've had more news."

"Yes, Brigadier. I was hoping to hear from you. There's something I want to say."

"Is there? Well, hold your horses," said Maxwell with the impatience of rank. "Look, he's dead."

"Dead. Who?"

"Hebbel, of course. Amazing, isn't it? Well, it saves a lot of fuss. Not the cyanide pill or anything dramatic like that. That's what I thought straight away. No, simple heart attack. Brought on by the excitement of being arrested, seems likely. It's really ironical!"

Goldsmith clutched the phone so tightly it hurt his hand.

"Was he interrogated at all? Did he make any statements?" he asked.

"Seems not. No, they got him to the police station and that was it. Dead on arrival at hospital. It's a strange business all round . . ."

"Could you hold on just a moment, Brigadier?" said Goldsmith.

He did not wait for a reply, but laid the phone on the desk and stood up. From this position all he could see from his window were clouds moving across a blue-grey sky, but a couple of paces brought other buildings and the crowded car-park into view. He paused at the window. The walls were painted white. It could be anything he wanted.

Then he strode rapidly out of the office.

Jenkinson looked up in surprise as the door of his room burst open.

"Sir?" he said, standing up.

"Have you done anything yet?"

"You mean, what you asked me to do just now?" asked Jenkinson looking justifiably aggrieved. "I'm sorry, but it was only a moment . . ."

"Good. Then forget it. All of it. Right?"

"Yes, sir. If you say so."

Without another word, Goldsmith picked up the J. T. Hardy's file which lay on the desk and returned to his own room.

Seated in his chair once more, he picked up the telephone.

"Sorry to go off so abruptly," he said, "but something came up. Now, you were saying about Hebbel . . .?"

"Yes. Well, it seems the fellow had settled down in the part of the country he'd been brought up in, and, listen to this, he was actually using his own name! Isn't that incredible? All that searching, and there he was!"

"Incredible," agreed Goldsmith.

"And, odder still, he was evidently a pillar of the community. Good family man, churchgoer, full of good works helping local charities, well loved by everyone. Created quite a stir when they came for him. And now he's dead, well, there'll be a bit of fuss locally."

"I'm sure they'll sort it out," observed Goldsmith.

"I'm sure. Still, it does make you wonder. Could it *all* be a front? What do you think, Goldsmith? Is it possible for a man like that to put his old self behind him? Could a man change so much?"

Goldsmith did not even pause to think.

"No," he said.

## About the Author

Reginald Hill has been widely published both in England and in the United States. Among his novels are *A Fairly Dangerous Thing* and *Another Death in Venice*, and in the famous Pascoe-Dalziel series, *Deadheads*, *Exit Lines*, *A Clubbable Woman*, *An Advancement of Learning*, and *An April Shroud* (all available in Signet). He lives with his wife in Yorkshire, England.

Coming Soon . . .
Red-hot Models and Cold-blooded Murder

# THINNING THE TURKEY HERD

A Jimmy Flannery Mystery
by Robert Campbell
Author of the Edgar Award-Winning *The Junkyard Dog*

---

*Tough Chicago Irishman Jimmy Flannery has a nose
for mayhem. As city sewer-inspector, he has to. So
when a killer sets out to prune the year's crop of
top models, Flannery is there to track the scent. But
before he's through, gorgeous Joyce Lombardi disap-
pears, an innocent man is lined up to take the fall
for a powerful political bigwig, and Flannery begins
to wonder if he has the stomach for it all . . .*

---

# There's an epidemic with 27 million victims. And no visible symptoms.

It's an epidemic of people who can't read.

Believe it or not, 27 million Americans are functionally illiterate, about one adult in five.

The solution to this problem is you... when you join the fight against illiteracy. So call the Coalition for Literacy at toll-free **1-800-228-8813** and volunteer.

## Volunteer Against Illiteracy. The only degree you need is a degree of caring.